Quarterback Sneak

Rangers Football
Book 2

Kameron Claire

Snuggle Whore Press, LLC

To all the Witty, Wicked & Wild Readers...
Never let them silence our Witty tongues,
Never let them shame our Wicked needs,
Never let them stop our Wild deeds.

Thank you for the love and support!

ROCKY MOUNTAIN
RANGERS

Chapter One
Declan

"You threw four touchdowns with a completion rating of seventy-two percent, passed for two hundred and eighty yards and rushed for eighty-five. Statistically, this is the best game of your professional career. How do you feel?"

I throw Bob the reporter a taunting raise of my brow. "How do you think I feel, man? I'm freaking awesome."

The room chuckles, and I catch the slow shake of my brother Deacon's head in the back of the room. I'm a thousand percent cockier than my older sibling, who paved the way for me in every way. I'm also a better quarterback, but again, his leadership and experience have helped me be the man I am today.

Still, I'm the baby brother—so I'm supposed to be a pain in the ass.

"But seriously, Bob. We've got a great team, so how can I not feel awesome? Our offensive line is the strongest it's ever been. Dave, Tyrel, Sakto and Aggie protect me, giving me the time I need to connect with Devlin, Jordan and Jennings. We're in sync—the guys know where I need them before I let the ball loose. And although it's easy to feel confident right now, we have fourteen more games left in the season and a long way to go. We're going to take it one game at a time."

A super cute blonde shifts in her chair, instantly capturing my attention. She's new here—not a member of the regular press crew stationed near Spring City—and familiar.

So fucking familiar that it takes me by surprise.

"What's your question?" I ask her, even though she didn't raise her hand, which causes everyone's gaze to swing her way.

Clearly taken aback by my attention, she bites her plump lip, which makes something within me swell. I can't help it. It's nature. A million years' worth of predator versus prey roaring to life inside of me.

I want to pounce—instinct deep inside poised to claim her as mine before I even know her name.

As is customary, she stands to be heard throughout the crowd. She's got a banging body—curves in all the right places—the way the buttons of her blouse stretch across her chest, telling me she's more than a handful. She's girl-next-door beautiful, subdued and yet arresting.

"Next week the team will face the number one ranked defense in the league. What's your plan to avoid becoming another one of Trayson Butler's sack statistics?"

And then it hits me. I don't know if it's her voice, or

the curve of her lips, or the twinkle in her eye, but I do know her name—and her smart, sexy, warm, and wet mouth.

Amelia Pruitt, the girl-next-door that got away from me my senior year in college.

What the hell is she doing at a Rangers football press conference?

Flashing her a taunting smile—the same one I used when I approached her at the clubhouse all those years ago—I answer. "I'm going to do what I do every week. Rely on my offensive line to protect me and get the ball in the air before Trayson has a chance to even blow a kiss in my direction." I throw her a wink for extra measure, something I'm sure my brother and father will chew my ass for later.

Don't flirt with the press.

That's almost always rule number one, but how can I not when one look at her brings back memories of a hot, decadent weekend right before Christmas break. Jesus, my body hardens with the thoughts as I watch her retake her seat and glance nervously at the reporters sitting around her.

Someone else raises their hand and I move on to another round of questions, but my gaze keeps coming back to Amelia with her pouty lips and dark chocolate eyes. She was unlike most girls who threw themselves at a guy like me in college. Super smart, she tutored a couple of my teammates who were at risk of failing some of their core classes—never once dating one of them or attending our notorious parties—except that one time when she did.

I remember that night with vivid clarity. Watching her walk into the clubhouse was like watching an untouched angel walk into the pits of Gomorrah. Her sweetness ensnared me and maybe I corrupted her that weekend—who am I kidding? I definitely corrupted her, exploring her body in every way imaginable—but it was the best damn weekend of my life and I've been chasing that feeling ever since.

I have full intentions of nabbing her credentials and her phone number after the game press conference ends, but I'm waylaid by my brother and father, who rush me into the training room. But before they push me into a conference room, I tell one of the many assistants roaming around to grab her card and invite her to the Wednesday family fun night we host twice a month.

"Who's the blonde filling in for Mike?" Deacon asks with a raise of his brow. We know Mike from the *Spring City Gazette* and now that Deacon points it out, I realize he's missing today.

"A woman I knew in college. Is she working for the Gazette? I didn't get her credentials."

"A woman you knew, huh?" A self-satisfied smirk spread across my brother's face. I've grown too predictable, my slut status well-known amongst my teammates and family.

"Focus!" our father snaps, leading us into a small, soundproof conference room.

"What's up, Pop?" I can't imagine what he's pissed about. We just played the best game of the season. ESPN will talk about us all week. Even our defensive line broke team and league records. What's there to be mad about?

"Aggie's soon-to-be ex-wife is threatening to go public with a domestic violence claim to include very graphic, hopefully Photoshopped, pictures. Deidre and our lawyer are talking to him now."

"Oh, shit." I exchange a glance with Deacon, who is shaking his head. We've all met Ellen, who has an explosive temper and is quick to throw hands despite her diminutive stature. I can't imagine Aggie laying a finger on her, but I know for a fact she's swung at him many times. Still, a DV claim must be taken seriously and as the team captain, as well as a Scott, I have no choice but to put on my business hat.

Our father continues, "Couple this with the strip club incident in Nashville a few weeks ago and the DUI last week and I'm putting a team gag order in place, as well as a curfew."

The vice-grip tightens around my throat. I hate being shackled, and a curfew will definitely fuck up my sex life. "The guys aren't going to like that."

He narrows his eyes and points a finger at me. "Maybe if the team acted their age and remembered they're adults—many of whom have wives and children— they wouldn't need a curfew. I shouldn't have to ask my players to keep their noses clean, but I will not have scandals rocking this organization, nor will I have conversations about our championship team overshadowed by tomfoolery."

My perpetual smile fades. Why do I feel like he's talking about me?

I shrug. "I'll talk to the team."

"No, Deacon and I will address the team with you standing in the front, taking the brunt of my anger as the team captain. The only reason I'm giving you notice is because you're also a Scott. This team is too good, and we have too much riding on this year, to screw it up with adolescent hijinks. No one talks to the press unless sanctioned by me, and no parties until we get Aggie past this. Understood?"

"Yeah."

"I don't think you do." My father, who rarely raises his voice, puts his finger in my face. "No blonde reporters, Declan. I'm serious. Keep it in your pants for a while."

My jaw drops open and I try the sweet and innocent bat of my eyelashes that works on our mother. "All I did was wink at an old friend from college."

"Yeah, right." Deacon chuckles, not even slightly fooled by me or my intentions.

"Stay away from her," my father mumbles as he exits the conference room.

I follow my father down the hall in lockstep with Deacon. We exchange a knowing glance and I know this is about more than a strip club brawl, a DUI by a third-string player, and an angry ex-wife. Deacon announced his engagement to a woman none of us knew about a few weeks ago and the local press has been eating the story up, desperate for more juicy details. Mostly, he's ignored their requests, letting the media sit with their questions and speculations while our sister Deidre handles the tabloids. Not even I know the real story about him and London Black, although I suspect it has something to do with the rumors that our granddad will retire soon, opening up his position for my father to fill, and ultimately the general manager slot for Deacon—which he has been training for since he stepped out of the huddle and turned over the quarterback and team captain reins to me.

So, there's a lot riding on the team this year and I get that, but my father should know that nothing is going to stop me from winning a championship ring this year. Not even a hot blonde with a banging body built for sin.

Nothing.

Chapter Two
Amelia

He doesn't remember me.

For the first time in a long time, I'm confident I made the right decision all those years ago by not telling him about his son. I've been sweating this press junket ever since Mike got injured, worried that an awkward encounter with Declan would ruin any chance of ever introducing them.

Filling in for Mike and running the sports column for the last few weeks has been an amazing opportunity—my first real chance to use my journalism degree at the Gazette, my name finally in a byline, although small and hidden underneath Mike's well-known name—but coming face-to-face with Declan Scott has been a nightmare brewing for over five years.

"Ma'am?" A guy twice my age chases me out of the building into the parking lot.

"Yes?"

"Declan Scott wants to talk to you." The name embroidered on his Rangers polo shirt is Brad.

"I'm afraid that's not possible."

Yeah, I bet he wants to talk to me. Declan Scott's sexual exploits are legendary. The list of women he's dated is impressive, if not downright nauseating. I wouldn't have thought I was his type in college—although our weekend together screams otherwise—but over the last few years he's proven he likes a wide variety of women.

And often.

"He's invited you to attend the family fun night this Wednesday."

"Why would he do that?"

"We invite all the press, ma'am. Considering you're new, the team wants to make sure you feel welcome." He shrugs and hands me an envelope with multiple passes. "Bring the family. Do you need more than four passes?"

Bring the family? So, this isn't Declan trying to get into my pants, but an honest-to-goodness perk of the job? "No. Four passes are perfect."

Danny, my five-year-old son, would love to attend a family fun night at the stadium. He's a huge football fan, although I doubt he understands the game. What he gets are the roaring fans, flashing lights and energy rolling off the TV. Attending a football event would be the highlight of his young life, and my brother Andrew would love it, too.

I don't know why I've turned them into Rangers fans. Maybe I wanted him to watch his father from afar, knowing one day I'll have to tell him who Declan is to him and hoping he'll have formed his own opinion of the man if that time comes.

When the time comes.

Jesus—even thinking about it makes me nauseous.

My senior year in college, I did the one thing I never do—I let loose and attended a clubhouse party. Between finals and the fear of my first Christmas at home without my father, I needed a distraction.

I found that distraction in Declan Scott.

Why he gave me a second look I'll never know, but that weekend I did things I've never done before or since. He encouraged me to act against my reserved nature by flashing his sinfully wicked smile and merely suggesting something might be fun.

Spoiler alert: it was all fun. Every dirty little filthy deed.

After that weekend, finals and Christmas break, I came back to school focused on graduating—figuring a future with Declan was simply out of the question. I mean, he was and is one of the most desired, sought after and eligible bachelors in the country.

I had an internship with the Denver NBC affiliate lined up, shadowing Ms. Justine Leonard, a prize-winning journalist. My future was set and although Declan gave me more orgasms that weekend than I'd had in my entire life, I couldn't risk my heart to the most popular guy in school who had his future mapped out, too.

Then, in late February, I realized something was

wrong. I'd skipped two periods and my iron-clad stomach was off. I don't know why pregnancy hadn't clicked before that moment, but when I took the test... well, let's just say, it was the first test I've ever failed.

For weeks, I debated what I should do. I made two appointments to terminate the pregnancy, always cancelling at the last minute. I stalked Declan at school intending to tell him, but he was always with his team-mates or a flock of women—neither of which seemed like an opportune moment to bring up a baby.

And then the *Sports Illustrated* article came out announcing Declan Scott as the professional league's new up-and-comer. He graced the cover of the national magazine as teams courted him and sponsors rushed to wine and dine him. Although his family owns a profes-sional team, with his older brother secure in the quarter-back position, Declan was looking to join another team where he could walk on to the starting position. I assumed he'd leave Colorado to pursue his dreams while I watched mine shrivel on the vine. I couldn't derail his future for a weekend fling even if I had every right to do so, and to be honest, I didn't want to become a wife to a man trapped by me or a baby.

Call me stupid, but my pride is too high to start a relationship with a man who doesn't want me for me.

I get in my car and look at the passes. They are open for the season from now until Christmas. I can't risk facing Declan with Danny in tow—just in case he recog-nizes me. Maybe I'll do a couple more interviews, and if he continues not to recognize me… well, that's a good thing, right?

Shit. I don't know.

I'm all jumbled up inside. Declan is as beautiful as I remember. I thought seeing him on TV for the last few years had desensitized me to any residual feelings I had for him, but ten seconds of his attention today and I'm as starstruck as ever. The weekend we spent together was wild and unexpected, as the college hero and notorious bad boy showed me a sweet and sinful side to his personality. He seduced me, but he also wooed me, making me fall head over heels in love without ever uttering a lie of adoration in return.

He never promised me more.

Never confessed feelings he didn't have.

We just clicked that weekend, and a part of my heart irrevocably became his.

After seeing him today, feelings I didn't think I had came rushing back.

Did I pine for and build a perfect image of the man because I was pregnant with his child? Possibly.

Or was it because our weekend together was the most passionate and complete sexual experience of my life? Probably.

No. I will definitely not be coming to Wednesday's family fun night, but I will continue to do my job, because in the end that's what matters. When I graduated college five months pregnant, I had to walk away from my internship at the NBC affiliate, and although I don't begrudge my son in any way—Danny is the light of my life—I want the career I'd worked to have before peeing on that stick.

And nothing is going to stop me.

Nothing.

"The team is six and two entering week nine. After your loss last Sunday to Seattle, you are now the number two rated team in the league. What went wrong?" a reporter asks.

I watch Declan fight to remain relaxed, but he fails miserably. Folding his arms over his broad chest, he leans back in his chair and shrugs his shoulders. "We had an off night and Seattle is a great team. I could say it had to do with the weather, or because the new moon had a mercury shadow over it or some shit, but the simple fact is, they showed up a little stronger and played a little harder and maybe they wanted it a little more than us. I'm not worried about our offensive or defensive lines, nor am I worried about the upcoming weeks. We're near halfway through the season and we're just getting into our groove. We're only going to get better."

"There's a lot of personal drama on the team this year that seems to pop up in between the record-breaking news clips. Do you think that is contributing to performance problems on the field?" a different reporter asks.

Declan narrows his eyes at the guy asking the question. "No, I don't think that has anything to do with anything. Next question."

I've been filling in for Mike for seven weeks now, and although Declan has made eye contact with me and even thrown me a wink a time or two, he's yet to call me by name or show me he knows who I am in any way whatsoever. Part of me is relieved. Part of me is heartbroken, but considering Mike will be back next week, Danny and I will be attending Wednesday's family fun night.

Declan's gaze scans over me as it always does, and although his eyes linger once again, there's no sign of recognition, which only solidifies my decision. I'm not sure if the passes expire once I turn in my press badge, but I don't want to deny my son or brother this opportunity. It's a memory that will stick with them forever.

The Rangers' family-focused vibe is top-notch. As soon as we pull into the parking lot, I see the staff and food vendors have set up a nice little carnival leading onto the practice field. There are probably a hundred people here, but my understanding is there could be upwards of two hundred fifty over the course of a few hours. Football players are often in attendance, but from what I'm told, it's normally only the players who have families of their own.

Declan Scott is not in attendance.

"Mommy, Mommy! I want to bounce in the bouncy house."

With us is my brother Andrew and my mother Vivian. Andrew is a couple of years older than me, but because of a traumatic brain injury he suffered as a young teenager, he still lives at home with my mother—which, after my father died, turned out to be a blessing. He lives in the mother-in-law's suite, detached from the house, so he has as much freedom as he can handle while still being close enough to where my mother can monitor him and vice versa.

Danny and I also live with my mother, but now that I have a full-time job with benefits, I hope to buy a house in the neighborhood soon.

"Danny, remember what we said? We have to eat before we play."

Andrew bumps me on the shoulder. "Why don't you get us food and I'll take him to the bouncy castle?"

My brother is great with Danny and I know he will give his life to protect him, but I still get nervous in crowds like this. I glanced at my mother, who nods her head, letting me know she'll keep an eye on both of them. "Okay, but be careful. I'll grab us some hotdogs and you grab a table near the fun."

Andrew swings Danny up into his arms without uttering another word and heads toward the carnival rides, my mother following behind them. On the practice field, some of the older kids are running drills with players—I presume third string—because how horrific would it be to have one of your star players injured while goofing around during the middle of the season?

All the food lines are long. The minutes tick by and the longer I go without seeing a Scott or anybody from the head office, the looser the bands across my chest get. I know someday I'll have to confront this, but my heart breaks with all the bad scenarios that could occur.

Declan has spent the last five years of his professional career being the consummate bachelor. Hot cars, hotter women, and the biggest and best parties. Nothing about him screams family man, so how will he respond on the day he learns he has a child? It's one thing for him to lash out at me—I'm sure he'll be angry and resentful, even suspicious—but my heart won't take him denying his child when Danny is at such an impressionable age. He's only now asking questions about his daddy and wondering why he's not around. Maybe once Declan matures and has a family of his own, he'll be more receptive to a relationship with his long-lost son.

I know I'm wrong for taking the decision away from Declan, but I can't risk breaking Danny's heart.

"Amelia Pruitt. The girl that ran away." A cannon ball drops into my stomach as the heat of his body presses against my back at the same moment his breath hits my ear.

I turn slowly and come face-to-face with blue eyes exactly like my son's. "Declan. I didn't think you recognized me."

"How could I forget you?"

"You never said anything."

"Yeah, with all the shit going on—the bad publicity and stuff—my father ordered me to stay away from you." He looks me up and down, his gaze hungry and reminiscent of the night we came face-to-face at the clubhouse. One look from him and my knees go weak. "You're still as beautiful as ever. Why couldn't I find you after Christmas break?"

"You were looking for me?" My eyes widen in surprise. All the time I stalked him, I never thought he was looking for me, too.

He tilts his head. "I kept an eye open, but I didn't see you in any of our classes, the library and, of course, you never came back to the house."

"You know very well that was a one-time thing." I lick my lips and look around, spotting Andrew and Danny busy at the carnival rides with my mother. I have to get rid of Declan before they come back. Although, knowing my brother, I'll have to tear him away from the games and bouncy castles once I have their food.

"It didn't have to be a one-time thing. I thought we had a good time that weekend. I would've liked to continue seeing you, but—"

"But—" I break in "—you had more than enough people clamoring for your attention and, to be quite honest, you were very busy the last couple of months of our senior year. If I remember correctly, you weren't even at graduation."

"True. I was at spring training camp."

"Exactly."

"So, probably not the most ideal time to start a relationship."

I scoff. I can't stop the wry snort from coming out of my lips. "Relationship? Relationships aren't your style."

Declan's eyes narrow on me. "Shacking up with a football player for the weekend isn't really your style and yet, that's exactly what happened."

Ouch. Okay, he has a point.

I cast my eyes to the ground and turn my back on him to step forward in the line. He takes a couple extra steps to stand in front of me, making himself unavoidable. The fans around us murmur his name, distracting him from the conversation at hand. He waves absentmindedly, grabbing a pen and signing an autograph or two without ever making eye contact with the people asking, then surprises me by grabbing my hand and pulling me out of line. "Come on."

I'm too shocked to protest and blindly follow him behind the food vendors to the tunnel entrance of the training facility, which is off limits to the fans.

"Where are we going?" My brain finally engages, and I dig my heels in, yanking my hand out of his.

"I'd like to talk to you without a lot of interruptions."

"What do you want to talk about?"

He lifts my left hand and kisses it. "I don't see a ring. I'm assuming you're not married."

"So what?"

"So, go out with me. Let's have the date we never got to have."

I shake my head. "I can't."

He frowns, but continues to hold my hand, his thumbs swiping back and forth gently—his touch seductively soothing. "I'm sorry I didn't get in touch with you sooner. If I knew you were in town, I definitely would've called. If I remember correctly, you were supposed to be working for NBC in Denver, not down here in Spring City. Look—I know Mike's coming back next week, which means you will not be in the press room and that's why I'm here tonight. I came here for you, Amelia. Go out with me. Let me take you to dinner."

Everything within me wants to say yes. The attraction I felt for him the first time I saw him is just as strong now as it ever was, but I know nothing good can come from him and me. Not if he's not ready for the baggage I come with.

His baggage.

Our beautiful baggage.

It's as if the Gods want to make sure this meeting happens. From behind me I hear Danny yelling, "Mommy, Mommy! You found the quarterback!"

Chapter Three
Declan

Amelia is even more beautiful than I remember. Being close to her lush body and breathing in her scent, images of her underneath, riding and bent over in front of me fill my head, causing everything within me to harden. But when a young child screams *Mommy*, her entire body tightens and eyes pop wide.

"Mommy?" I say right before a young boy with piercing blue eyes runs up and throws himself around her legs. On instinct, Amelia bends down and picks up the little boy, straddling him on her hip.

"Mommy, Mommy! How'd you... how'd you know the quarterback?"

Amelia is white as a ghost as she looks at me and turns her body so the child straddling her hip is as far away as possible.

"Who is this?" I say as casually as possible, but deep down—my God—I fucking know.

Those blue eyes are Scott eyes.

Just like mine.

Just like my father's.

The little boy's cherub face brightens with my question. "My name is Declan Daniel, but you can call me Danny."

"Declan?" My brows shoot up. "But that's my name."

"No... your name is Scott and you're the quarterback."

"That's right, I am." My eyes bounce back-and-forth between him and Amelia, who looks like she wants to peel off her skin right now. "How old are you, Danny?"

The little boy puts up his hand, showing me all five fingers. My gut twists and I'm on the verge of throwing up.

Another man runs up behind her, looking from me to Amelia to Danny and back to me. "Holy shit. You're Declan Scott. I wish I had something for you to sign."

Amelia looks like she's about to bolt and I can't allow that. Not when she's holding a child that I am 99.9% sure is mine. I don't know who this guy is—if he's a boyfriend or something else—but I can't let her leave without us having a conversation.

An almost-six-years-overdue conversation.

"You know what, man? You seem like a genuine fan, so I will tell you what we're going to do. Let's go back into the training facility where I have a couple of things to give you and Danny."

Amelia shakes her head. "I don't think that's a good idea."

I wrap my fingers around her bicep, the one not wrapped around our child, and lead her down the tunnel. "I insist."

"This is awesome!" The enthusiastic thirty-something-year-old man is practically skipping next to us.

I whisper to her. "Who is this guy, Amelia? A boyfriend?"

"This is my brother Andrew."

Brother. I can work with that.

"How are you doing?" I turn to him and offer him my hand. He shakes it and there's something about him I can't quite put my finger on. He has the body of a thirty-year-old, but the excitement and demeanor of a teenager.

"Oh, my God. This is the coolest thing that has ever happened to me!" And then, without warning, he turns and runs in the opposite direction, exclaiming, "We forgot Mom!"

"Andrew!" Amelia yells after him.

I grab her arm again, holding her in place. "I'll take care of it."

I motion to one of the security guards and point at the guy running down the hall. "Help that guy find his mother and then bring them to the conference room in the training suite on the second floor."

"Yes, sir." The security guard jogs after Andrew.

"This will give us a couple of minutes to talk."

Amelia halts our progress right before the elevators, smoothing back Danny's blond hair. Her voice is shaky, and I suspect her emotions are shredded. "We can't. Not right now. Not in front of my family. Declan, please."

I look her deep in the eye, purposely moving my gaze to Danny, who giggles and kicks his feet—intent on running down the hallway after his uncle. "Say yes or no, Amelia. Right now. Yes or no? Tell me the truth."

Tears fill her eyes as she looks at Danny, kissing his forehead before setting him down on his feet. He instantly dances around—a boy of five with the energy to match—oblivious to the tension thickening the air between us. She licks her lips and nods her head imperceptibly. "Yes."

I exhale the breath I'm holding and shake my head. "How could you not have told me?"

"We can't get into that right now. Please. My mother doesn't know."

Danny takes that moment to squeal Andrew's name and takes off down the long corridor towards his uncle and a woman I can only assume is their mother. "Fine, but we talk about this tomorrow night."

"Okay."

"I'm serious, Amelia. You can't hide from me this time and you owe me an explanation."

"Yes. Tomorrow night. Wherever you want, Declan. But please, for right now, just be the star quarterback who's super nice to his fans."

I see the fear in her face, the overwhelming emotion threatening to break free, so I take a step back and simply nod. "Fine."

"Declan! Where's your head?" Greg, the offensive coordinator, yells from the sideline.

"Up my ass, apparently," I mumble to myself. I got shit for sleep last night and my appetite is nonexistent, which is less than ideal when I burn a couple thousand calories during practice. I've gone through a million emotions since looking into Danny's big blue eyes yesterday.

Anger, definitely, but also remorse, indignation, suspicion, and profound sadness.

I don't know what Amelia is going to say when we meet this evening, but I have to believe my demeanor over the years did not give her the confidence that presenting me with a child would go over well.

How can she think so little of me?

Can I blame her?

Sure, we had a crazy sex-filled weekend with little knowledge of each other beforehand and no contact afterward, so I guess I can't be angry at her for not telling me.

And yet, I am.

What kind of bastard must my child think I am considering I've never come to visit?

I've never been there to celebrate his birthday.

I've never given him a Christmas present.

Amelia had said she was on birth control, not that I

think the weekend would have gone differently if she hadn't been. Maybe I would have been a bit more careful, but probably not. If she was looking to trap me, she could have done it five years ago. There's no way my family will not accept and support my child—and I don't need a DNA test to know he's mine.

He looks exactly like me.

My mother is going to lose her shit when she finds out.

My whole family is going to freak.

And I thought Granddad was unhappy about Deacon's quickie engagement. This might put the old man in his grave.

Then there is the question of how Amelia feels about me. She went through a pregnancy on her own. She's raised our child for five years—on her own. Was I such a bastard that she didn't think she could come to me? Did she think I would force her to do something she didn't want to do? I know we didn't know each other before that weekend, but if that's the vibe I'm sending out into the universe, I need to do a serious overhaul of the public's perception of me.

Now you know why I didn't sleep last night.

"I need a break." I jog over to Greg and throw the football to Nathan, my backup, who instantly runs onto the field.

"What's going on?"

"Nothing. I didn't sleep last night, and I need a break. Everything's fine." Famous last words.

"Hit the showers and go home. Are you in pain? Do

you need something to help you sleep?" Greg raises his brow.

"No. Just a break. I'll see you tomorrow." I grab my helmet and walk down the tunnel to the locker rooms. On my phone sits a text message from Amelia.

Any chance we can meet earlier? I'm a basket case and can't concentrate on work.

She sent it almost an hour ago. Call it a perverse pleasure, but I'm glad this is tearing her up as much as it is me.

Yeah. Let me take a shower and then I'll head your way. What's your address?

Three bubbles instantly appear.

No. You can't come to the house. Not yet. You can pick me up at the Gazette or I can meet you somewhere.

I'll ping you as I'm pulling up to the building.

Something tells me I want her trapped in my car. If this conversation gets heavy—and how could it not?—I don't want her to walk away.

Twenty minutes later, I'm watching a leggy blonde—the kind that would attract me no matter what—walk toward my car through fresh eyes. This is the mother of my child, not just a babe in a skirt.

Although I have to wonder, why can't she be both?

Fuck, maybe I have been a douchebag all these years.

I jump out of the driver's seat and swing around the hood, opening the passenger door.

She throws me a small smile. "Hi."

"Hey." Any other woman, any other time, I'd flash her a big smile and lean in for a kiss. But considering the circumstances bringing us together today, I'm betting she would find that inappropriate. And yet, I still kind of want to do it. Closing her door, I walk slowly around the hood, thinking about what I should say first. I can't believe how nervous I am—my palms are sweating, and my heart is racing.

I slip into the driver's seat and drive down the road, the quiet between us deafening with all that is unsaid.

Finally, Amelia breaks the silence. "Where are we going?"

"My condo." I glance at her as I pull up to a red light. "I figure the conversation will be difficult and warrants privacy."

She nods, her eyes going to her hands in her lap.

Luckily, my condo is only a few blocks from the *Gazette's* downtown office, so we're pulling into my parking space in a matter of minutes. We exit the vehicle and ride the elevator up to the penthouse in silence. Shaggy, the sheepdog, greets us as soon as the doors open.

Amelia gasps and drops to her knees. "Oh my god, he's so cute."

"Yes, she is. This is Shaggy, or Shaggerella when she's acting like a princess." I purse my lips together, trying to tamp down the first of many questions dancing on my tongue.

Shit, I can't stop the words from tumbling out of my mouth. "Does Danny like dogs?"

Amelia's loving on Shaggy but looks up at me with a smile on her perfect lips. "He loves them."

Happiness swells in my heart and tightens my chest. I nod and run my hand through my hair, walking past them into the kitchen. "Would you like something to drink?"

"Wine?" She stands and brushes the fur from her skirt.

"Good idea." I grab two bottles and place them on the island. "Red or white?"

"White, please."

Opting for a beer myself—which I usually shun during the season because of the bloat—I pour her a glass. I'd love to do a shot to calm my nerves, but that would be immature of me, and I feel like every move I make, every word I say, is being analyzed and catalogued for review. "I'd like to start this conversation by apologizing."

Amelia stops with her wine glass raised to her lips. "You're apologizing to me?"

I shrug and motion to the loveseat, waiting until we're comfortable at opposite ends. "We had a super-hot weekend together, but I obviously left you with the impression I'm a bastard if you found out you were pregnant and didn't come to me with it."

She closes her eyes and shakes her head. "It's not like that, Declan. You had your future mapped out. There were a half-dozen teams champing at the bit to sign you, as well as sponsors flying you all over the country to wine and dine you. It wasn't until late February I learned I was pregnant and then I spent the next couple of weeks debating what I was going to do about it. I thought about talking to you, but in the end, I didn't want to disrupt your plans."

I clench my jaw, anger simmering in my belly. "I don't know how to respond to that, Amelia. You should have told me. Now I have a five-year-old son I don't know, who also doesn't know me, and I'll never get those years back."

"And I don't know what you want me to say, Declan, other than I'm sorry." A tear falls down her cheek.

God dammit. I can't handle seeing a woman cry. I reach out and grab her hand, interlacing our fingers. "Will you tell me about him? Who does he think I am?"

"He thinks you're the Rangers' quarterback, the best player in the league and the guy in the insurance commercials. He loves those commercials and thinks you're hilarious."

I don't know why, but that cuts me deep. My son knows me, but he doesn't know me. "Who does he think his father is? Does he ask about him?"

She nods. "He's been asking more and more lately. I think it's because he's in kindergarten and is being influenced by the other kids."

"What do you tell him?"

"I told Danny his father has a very demanding career

that causes him to travel a lot and then I distract him with something else."

Now I close my eyes and shake my head in disbelief. "And that works?"

"It did." She glances down at our joined hands. "It hasn't lately."

"So, what was your plan? Were you ever going to tell him about me or me about him?" I'm getting upset again, and I do my best to tamp down my anger at her and myself.

"Yes. No. I don't know." She pulls her hand out of mine and jumps to her feet, walking around to pace the space between me and the windows. "I thought once you settled down and started a family I'd come to you with this."

"What?" That is the most ridiculous thing I've ever heard. "Why wait until then?"

"Because then I'd know you were ready to be a father." She stares out the windows with her back to me, giving me nothing more to go on.

Glaring at her back, I also stand and walk back into the kitchen. I grab myself another beer and the wine bottle, bringing both back to the table. "Will you introduce us and tell him who I am?"

She turns slowly to face me. "Exactly what kind of relationship are you asking for, Declan?"

"I'm his father. He's my flesh and blood, Amelia. I want to have the relationship a father and son should have." I hand her the wineglass.

She takes it and sucks back the contents, as if she

needs liquid courage. "Please understand. The only thing worse for Danny than not knowing his father is knowing his father doesn't want him. If you come into his life, Declan, it's forever. Don't start this relationship if you don't want to make the commitment."

Chapter Four
Amelia

The look on Declan's face lets me know my words have gutted him.

"I wouldn't do that, Amelia. If you had come to me in the beginning, I would've done the right thing. I would've taken care of you and Danny. For Christ's sake, he's heir to the Scott family fortune. I should've been taking care of him the entire time."

"This isn't about money, Declan. Danny is the sweetest little boy with a huge heart and while I would love for you to be a part of his world, I want to make sure you understand this is for life. You will break his heart if you change your mind in a couple of weeks."

"I'm not going to change my mind. Although my actions over the years might say otherwise, I can be mature. I care about other people's feelings." He stands up and walks over to me, enveloping me in his arms before I understand what's happening. Maybe he can sense I'm on the edge of falling apart, but I melt into his hug despite being the most scared I've ever been.

I'm going to let him into Danny's world and his heart and pray for the best.

"I know this is scary, but I promise I will bust my ass to be the father Danny deserves. If you've ever wanted for anything, you'll never want for it again. You have a seat at every home game, and I'll figure out how to balance football and family. I mean, a bunch of guys do it, so it has to be possible."

I chuckle, wrapping my arms around his waist. His body is warm and solid, sparking to life old carnal feelings I can't think about right now. This is about our son and nothing else. I push Declan back gently and take a step away, wiping the tears on my face. "Can I use your bathroom?"

He cups my cheek and rubs his thumb over the spot I just wiped clean with my hand, his bright blue eyes burrowing into mine. The look on his face says he wants to say more, so much more, but then he nods and takes a step back. "Yeah. It's down the hallway to the left."

Declan takes me home early so I can talk to my mom and he can talk to his family before we meet tomorrow for an afternoon at the playground—Danny's favorite spot. He squeezes my hand as he rolls to a stop in front of the *Gazette* building. "This is going to be good; I promise."

I nod and smile, pushing down all of my fears. It's not that I don't trust Declan to treat Danny well, but he's walking into a five-year-old's life with no experience of how to be a father. I've been doing this all along and I still find being a parent overwhelming some days. What's it going to be like for Declan as the youngest in his family with no nieces or nephews to have practiced on?

"I'll talk to you tomorrow and send you the address to the park."

"Sounds perfect."

"We agree? We'll hang out for a couple hours and maybe get a bite to eat before we talk to him about who you are?"

"Yes, Amelia. I know you're nervous, and I am too, but I'm also excited. I promise I won't do anything to upset Danny."

I flash him a genuine smile this time because I believe him. "Okay. I'll see you tomorrow."

I let myself out of the car and walk through the lobby to the elevators, taking it down to the garage. How am I going to explain this to my mother? Andrew will be excited, but my mother? She thinks Danny's father is some random boy I met one night at the college bar and has no idea I've known who Danny's biological father is all along.

We live on the northwest side of town in an older community with large yards and single-floor ranchers. There are big mature trees to hang tire swings from, and occasionally a tree is retrofitted with a makeshift playhouse that should have been demolished years ago. When I thought about the future, I saw myself buying a house nearby so my mother can help me with Danny and, as she got older, I'd be close enough to help her and Andrew.

I know someday Andrew will be in my care and I'm okay with that. Between him and my son, I've been reluctant to date over the years, knowing I come with a lot of baggage that most men will not want to take on.

But honestly, deep down, I know that is a lie. I think what really held me back was this day. In my head, I couldn't fathom entering a relationship before Danny and his biological father met, leaving the complication of another man being called Daddy out of the equation.

My mother sits on the couch with a blanket laid across her lap and looks up from her book when I walk through the front door. "You're home early."

"Yeah, we finished quicker than I thought we would." She thought I was working late on a project. "Where is Andrew?"

"His place. I think he's playing video games."

I nod. "Is Danny asleep?"

"He went down twenty minutes ago." She arches her brow. "You're not going to wake him, are you? He has school tomorrow."

"No, I'm not going to wake him. Look Ma, we need to talk."

She sets her book down and pulls off her glasses. "What's the matter, Ames?"

I kick off my shoes and sit down next to her, pulling

my knees up to my chest like I did when I was a kid. "It's about Danny's biological father."

My mom stares at me for a moment, her expression unreadable. "It's Declan Scott, isn't it?"

My jaw drops. "How could you possibly know that?"

She rolls her eyes. "Oh, please. First, you've always made a point of having Danny watch every televised Rangers game. Second, I saw you yesterday. You were a nervous wreck around him. Then, I remembered you went to the same university. I always assumed you had a crush on Declan, but after getting up close and personal with him yesterday and looking into his brilliant blue eyes that look exactly like Danny's, something told me he was the one. Now the question for you is, why didn't you tell me?"

Laying my forehead against the top of my knees, I sigh. "I don't know. I guess I was scared. He's an athletic superstar from a very rich and well-established family, and I was afraid he wouldn't want his child. Then there is the question of his family, who are rich and powerful enough to take Danny from me. I couldn't risk any of those scenarios, no matter how ridiculous they might be."

My mother frowns. "Does he want to meet his son?"

I nod, a small smile splitting my lips. "Very much so."

"And what about his family?"

I shrug. "I don't know yet. He's going to talk to them tonight like I'm talking to you now. I don't know how they're going to respond, considering the season and the championship and everything else going on. This is just one more thing, you know."

"Danny is not one more thing. He is everything."

"Of course, you and I know that, but I know very little about the Scott family outside of their money and close-knit decorum. They hold everything very close, avoiding scandal for decades—amazingly enough. I assume they are good people, but who knows?"

My mom pulls the blanket off of her lap and folds it carefully into a square, silence descending between us. She places it on the cushion and then pats it gently before standing up to stretch. "Well, if the Scott family sucks, we'll keep doing what we've always done and give Danny the best family we can give him."

I stand up, too, and wrap my arms around my mother's shoulders. "Thank you for always being there for me, Mom."

"I wouldn't have it any other way, baby girl."

Chapter Five
Declan

I try Deacon first, but the call goes straight to voicemail. Then I call Deidre, who answers on the second ring, slightly out of breath.

"Yell-ow." She pants.

"Did I reach you at a bad time?" I suspect she's dating my offensive lineman, Aggie, but I have absolutely no proof to back that up. Honestly, I don't want to know. If I did, I'm not sure who I would be more mad at. Him for dating my sister, or her for dating my best friend, who is a giant marshmallow on the inside. I don't think he can handle someone like her, and after his terrible divorce, I don't want to see him hurt by her.

Not that my sister is a bad person, but she's a corporate-level ball-buster, so what could she see in his giant gooey ass?

"Other than running on the treadmill through the Canadian Rockies, no."

I merge my BMW onto the two-lane highway leading

out of Spring City and north of Starlite Park. "Are you alone?"

"Who would be here with me?" she taunts, as if she knows my suspicions and finds teasing me with them enjoyable.

"I'm on my way over."

"What's up? Are you okay?" I hear her walking through her house, sipping on her water bottle.

"Yes. No. I don't know. I'm calling Mom and Dad and asking them to meet me at your house."

"Uh, why?"

"Because I don't want to deal with Granddad right now and you know how he miraculously appears whenever we have family business to discuss."

"Fine. I'll jump in the shower. Come on in when you arrive."

"Thanks." I hang up with her and call the house—probably one of the few landlines still in existence—and pray my mother is the one to answer the phone.

"Hello?" Her voice is sweet, as always.

"Hey. Where's Granddad?"

"Upstairs, I believe. Would you like me to get him?"

"No. Can you grab Dad and sneak over to Deidre's? I'm on my way right now."

"Uh, okay. We'll see you soon." I love my mom. She knows when to ask questions and when not to.

I also love my granddad, but he's old school and way more opinionated than I want to deal with right now. When Deacon brought London home for dinner a month or so ago, my granddad spent the next few weeks asking questions about her—none of which I knew the answer to —and then told me he was hiring a retired detective to investigate her. I don't know if he ever did that, but it wouldn't surprise me if he did. He's positive people are after our family fortune, and maybe some people are, but I don't think London with her unconventional looks is one of them.

Once Granddad hears I have a child, he'll demand a paternity test, even though Danny looks like my mini-me. I can't deal with that kind of negativity at this moment. I'm barely hanging on as it is, a sort of mania coursing through my veins. After my talk with Amelia, I'm excited about my future outside of football.

Was I looking to be a dad overnight? No.

Am I going to do everything I can to make up for lost time and be the best fucking father I can? Absolutely.

Am I also thinking about ways to woo Amelia into giving me another chance? Also, yes. Holding her in my arms earlier, something inside me came alive, and I didn't even know that raw need was dormant. Like a grinch, I felt my heart thump in my chest as I pulled her close, doubling when she wrapped her arms around me.

I should have known she was the one all those years ago.

She's still the one now.

I drive down Deidre's long driveway and park in front of her house, my parents rolling up in their golf cart behind me. Deidre's house is on the same plot of land as my parents—even though it's subdivided—and they can drive the trails through the garden to her house with very little off-road action.

"Hey son. Is everything okay?" My father raises his brow.

"Honestly? It's fantastic, but it's going to be quite a shock to the system, so let's go inside."

We enter Deidre's Mediterranean-style home to find her mixing drinks at the bar nestled in the corner of her sunken living room near the open patio doors.

"Your cryptic phone call made me think drinks are warranted."

"Warranted and necessary." I take a Scotch on the rocks from her and down it in one giant gulp.

My mother shares a look with Deidre and takes a sip of her vodka tonic. "Declan, what's going on?"

No reason to drag this out any longer. "You are grandparents to a beautiful five-year-old boy."

"What?" My mother squeaks.

"Holy shit," Deidre mutters, covering her mouth with her drink.

"God dammit, Declan!" My father sputters uncharacteristically. "Who? When? How could you be so reckless? Is she hitting you up for child support?"

"No. Nothing like that." I wave my hands, urging him to sit down and listen. "Remember the blonde reporter I said I knew in college?"

My father's eyes go to the sky, as if he's trying to recount all the hot blonde reporters that come to our facility. "Week three. The same night Aggie's ex-wife threatened to go public with the photos."

"Yes, that blonde."

"Declan, start explaining." My mother's voice wavers with emotion.

I hand Deidre my empty glass and slump into one of the patio chairs. "She came to the family fun night on Wednesday. I also went, fully intent on asking her out because I knew Mike was coming back and she'd no longer come to the press conferences. Then this little boy with my eyes—" I point at my father "—your eyes came running up, and she didn't have to say a word. I knew. I mean, he looks just like me."

I glance at my mom. "You know that photo you have of me at four on the mantle?"

She nods.

"Mirror fucking image."

"If you found this out yesterday, why are you only telling us now?" my father asks.

"When I met him yesterday, Amelia confirmed it, but asked me not to talk about it in front of her family. I guess she never told her mother it was me, and because of my aloofness at the press conference, she thought I didn't remember her anyway. However, we met today—like twenty minutes ago—to talk it out."

Deidre narrows her eyes. "So, was she never going to tell you about your child?"

I can see the wheels spinning in my sister's head. First and foremost, my sister is strapped to protect the family and the organization. If I was to tell her Amelia is a threat to me or us, my sister would go to war regardless of a cute five-year-old standing between us.

I shake my head and slide my hand down my face. "She was scared."

"Scared of what?"

I sigh. "We had a very hot active weekend right before Christmas, our senior year. After the break, I was jetting around the country talking to different teams and by the time she found out she was pregnant... well, let's just say my actions over the years haven't given the impression I have any desire to be a father."

"That's for sure." Deidre rolls her eyes.

"Shut up, Buster."

She hands me a fresh drink and chuckles, completely unaffected by any name I call her.

"From the limited interaction I saw of her with our child, she's an amazing mother and she's more worried about me not taking the role seriously than anything else. She doesn't want to break his heart."

My mother and father exchange a look and then interlace their fingers, as if they're holding on for dear life. "What's his name?"

"Declan Daniel, but he goes by Danny."

My mom clasps her free hand over her mouth as Deidre shakes her head. "She named him after you and yet hasn't found one opportunity in five years to tell you about him?"

I wave away her anger. "I've already gone through every fucking emotion you can have associated to this. Amelia fucked up by keeping him from me, but I believe she did it for the right reasons. Or at least the reasons that made sense to her at the time. She said the only thing worse for Danny than not knowing who his father is, is knowing who he is and that he doesn't want him. She said she'd introduce us tomorrow as long as I'm serious and understand this is a lifetime commitment."

"Are you ready to make that commitment?" my father asks.

"Yes." My eyes snap to his. Like not making the commitment is an option?

"Even if it cost you the championship?" he continues.

"I don't see what one has to do with the other. Lots of quarterbacks win championship rings and have families waiting for them at home."

"Family? What are you saying?" Deidre eyes pop wide.

"I'm saying Amelia is the girl that got away. Tomorrow, I'm going to meet my son and the three of us are going to spend time together. If I get a hint there can be more with her, I'm going for it. I've already lost five years. I'm not going to lose any more time than is absolutely necessary."

"What is it with our sons?" My father turns to my mother. "Why is it always all or nothing with them?"

My mother closes her eyes and shakes her head. "I guess when they know, they know. You were the same way, if I remember correctly."

"That was different. Time was different back then."

She scoffs. "It was the eighties, which wasn't that long ago. According to your own admission, you saw me across the quad and, without even knowing my name, knew you were going to marry me. As soon as that thought hit your head, nothing else mattered, including my feelings on the subject."

I stand up and walk to where they're sitting, crouching down, and placing my hand over theirs. "I know this is a shock but tell me you support me in this."

"Of course, we support you." My mom smiles up at me. "Now when can I meet my grandson?"

Deidre claps her hands together. "I'm finally an aunt!"

I chuckle. "Let me meet them tomorrow and I'll see what I can do. I'm not even sure we're going to tell him who I am tomorrow, and he definitely cannot meet you until after he knows me and is good with it."

"You know, the press is going to have a field day with this." Deidre sits on the other couch across from our parents.

I stand and shrug. "Fuck em."

She frowns. "We have to take this seriously, Declan. They're either going to paint you as an absentee piece of shit or her as some opportunistic female trapping the Rangers' star quarterback. Either way, they'll want to know why they're only learning about Amelia and Danny now when it's clear your son is five years old."

Even though I know she's right, that the press could say anything negative about her or my child brings about all my protective instincts. "It's none of their fucking business why I'm only telling them about them now. Do what you do, Deidre. Take care of it."

Chapter Six
Amelia

Danny and I pull up to the park at four, my little boy a bundle of excited energy with no idea of what's coming. To my surprise, Declan is already here, sitting on a park bench with a backpack and a group of teenagers surrounding him.

I unfasten Danny from his car seat and hold his hand as we walk through the parking lot to the playground. Declan's eyes watch us as he smiles and wraps up a couple of autographs for the teenagers. He stands and grabs the backpack, walking towards us.

"Hey." He smiles.

"Hey yourself." I fried my nerves fretting about this all night, and the emotions coursing through my veins cause my voice to squeak.

"Mommy! It's the quarterback," Danny says while jumping up and down.

I laugh. "It sure is, honey."

Declan gets down on one knee, so he's eye to eye with

Danny. "Hey, little man. Funny seeing you here."

"We're gonna play on the swings!"

"Oh, yeah?" He quirks his eyebrow. "I happen to love the swings."

"Do you want to push me high?"

He smiles. "I would love that."

Declan falls in beside me as we follow Danny to the swing set. "How was your day?"

I chuckle, because I know he's trying to fill the awkward space between us, which means he's just as nervous as I am. "It was good. And you? You got out of training early today."

"Yeah, Greg is going to kill me if I ask for another break." He sighs and runs his hand through his thick sandy blond hair. "I was wondering, if everything goes well today, how would you feel about bringing Danny to the game on Sunday? I have four passes for you. You'd sit in the family box with my mother and sister."

I bite my lip, a ball of nerves fluttering to life in my belly. "Uh..."

"We can discuss it later." Declan hands me the backpack, then helps Danny get on the swing. "How high do you want to go?"

Danny giggles and exclaims the same thing he always says. "To the moon!"

Like all five-year-olds, Danny's attention span lasts a few minutes before he moves on to something else. It takes no time for him to be over the swings and running to play on the jungle gym, which gives Declan and me a chance to move over to a bench and talk.

"So, how'd it go with your family?" I ask, pulling a juice out of my bag to prepare for when Danny comes running back to tell me he's thirsty.

Declan's eyes are glued to his son, but he turns his body toward me. "It went... well, there was every emotion you can imagine in a short period. But my mother and sister are excited to meet you and Danny. They asked me to invite you to the game on Sunday. My mother thinks it might be more comfortable if it's just you girls. I'll be on the field, of course. My father and brother as well. But we would tag up with you afterward for a family meet and greet."

I shake my head. "This is all so surreal."

"It's probably going to be weird for a while, but my parents are good people, and they just want a chance to get to know their grandson."

"Mommy!" Danny comes running up. "I want my juice."

"I figured you would." I smile and hand him his juice with a straw already in it.

"Are you having fun?" Declan smiles and scoots over to allow Danny to climb onto the bench between us.

"Yeah, did you see me on the slide?"

Declan nods. "I sure did. You are amazing, bud."

"Do you think you could teach me to throw a football like you?"

I see the look that comes over Declan's face—a combination of pride and unadulterated joy. "I sure can. Actually, I got you a present if your mom is okay with that."

"Can I have a present, Mommy?"

"Of course, you can."

Declan opens up the backpack and pulls out a small foam football, handing it to Danny. I don't know what it is about this moment, but tears fill my eyes as I watch my little boy—our little boy—bounce up and down with his hands wrapped around the ball.

"Look, Mommy. It's a football."

The grin on my face almost matches Danny's. "It sure is."

"Do you want to go onto the field and pass the ball back and forth until you're hungry?" Declan stands and waits for us.

Danny jumps off the bench and runs onto the field. "Yes!"

"I was going to run this past you before he came back. I hope this is okay."

"It's great. I'm grateful you're starting him off with something lightweight and, hopefully, pain-free."

"Of course." Declan throws me a wink and then chases Danny onto the field. Danny laughs as Declan sweeps him up in his arms and spins him in the air before setting him back down.

Watching Danny play with his father fills my heart with love, gratitude, and a bit of sadness.

Hope for a future where Danny has both a loving mother and a loving father to watch out for him fills me. Seeing this scene unfold makes me regret not getting in touch with Declan sooner, because he's absolutely right. He's missed the first five years of his son's life and he's never going to get that back.

Chapter Seven
Declan

I've been around my fair share of kids, mostly in a football capacity, and maybe it's because he's my son, but Danny is the sweetest, happiest, and most polite little boy I've ever met. Amelia has done an amazing job raising him on her own—although I suppose her mother helped—and I find myself attracted to her on more than just a physical level.

We toss the ball back and forth a few times, but Danny seems to find it more fun to run full speed toward me with the ball clutched against his chest. Half the time, I tackle him, picking him up and swinging him in the air, which causes him to giggle with immense glee. The other half, I let him take me to the ground, rolling to ensure he's always straddling my chest. He seems to like this even more.

"Danny, be careful with the quarterback. You don't want him to miss a game because you play too rough, do you?"

"No, Mommy."

I glance up at her and smile. "He's giving me quite the work out."

"Yeah, and you're getting him at the end of the day when he's tired. Just imagine what he's like in the morning." Amelia casts me a beautiful smile—not a hint of resentment in her tone—and a tinge of regret hits my chest, reminding me I might not see him often, depending on how he reacts to the news that I'm his father.

"Are you hungry, bud?"

"Yes!" Everything this little guy does is pure excitement and I'm here for it. I was the same way, and I wonder if he's been like that his entire life.

"What's your favorite food?" I ask, tucking the football back into the backpack I brought for him. Inside are a few more Rangers things I asked my sister to grab from our PR stash. By Sunday, my kid will have one of everything we make for five-year-olds.

"Pizza. No! Nuggets."

"What do you suggest, Mom?" On instinct, I place my hand on the small of her back as we walk like a family toward the parking lot.

Although she stiffens at first, I don't remove my hand, waiting until she eases into it.

"We don't normally do fast food on school nights and we only have soda once a week, but I guess we can do it today instead of tomorrow." She smiles down at Danny. "Do you want to go to Big Boys and get nuggets?"

Danny jumps up and down. "Yay!"

"I guess that settles it." I chuckle. "Let's eat some nuggets."

As we cross the parking lot and stop between our cars, Danny blurts, "I want to ride with the quarterback!"

Before I can say anything, Amelia is shaking her head.

"I don't have a car seat, bud. You can't drive with me today, but I promise I'll get one and give you and your mom a ride soon. Okay?"

He frowns and casts his eyes to the ground, responding with a meek "Okay," and it absolutely guts me.

I look at Amelia, who shakes her head, smiles, and mouths, "He's fine."

Fifteen minutes later, we're settled at the restaurant that's family-friendly with a sport bar vibe. We're sitting in a booth towards the back, but I get stopped by a couple of people who shake my hand, wish me luck and ask for autographs.

"I'm sorry. I should've remembered this place is sports heavy." Amelia grins as I finally take my seat.

"No worries. I don't mind signing autographs for fans."

Danny has his menu and crayons. He draws on the paper, fully occupied for the moment. My eyes keep bouncing between him and Amelia. I see so much of myself in him. The big blue eyes, the loud and outgoing personality, but I also see her. He's got her cute button nose, blond hair, and a dimple in his left cheek.

We place our orders, my mind whirling with questions, my nerves frayed by those same questions. How do I bring up this topic hanging over our heads? Maybe I don't. There's no reason to force Danny's parentage on him today. I can take time to get to know him and Amelia, while letting them get to know me.

As if Danny can feel the tension building at the table, he lifts his head and arches his brow. "What's your name?"

"My first name? It's Declan."

"Like me."

"Yep."

"Mommy, why does he have the same name as me?"

Amelia's jaw drops. She grabs her water and takes a deep drink before clearing her throat. "Well, Danny. I named you after your daddy."

His little brow furrows, and he stares at his drawing for a few seconds—long enough for me to cast Amelia a worried look. She smiles, but it doesn't reach her eyes, and she reaches out to brush his hair back. "What are you thinking, baby?"

"You named me after my daddy?" He looks at me. "And your name is the same as my name, so does that mean you're my daddy?"

"Would that be okay?" I ask, my heart heavy in my chest.

He shrugs and returns to his drawing and crayons. "I guess so. Where have you been?"

I glance at Amelia, who once again turns ashen. "Well, Danny, Declan didn't—"

I can't let her take the heat on this one. She's a

fantastic mother and I don't want him to be mad at her for not telling me when the situation is significantly more complicated than a five-year-old brain can handle. "Your mommy loves you so much that she wanted to make sure I could be a good daddy before she introduced us. She's very smart and protective of you."

"Yeah, she is." He glances up and pins me with his blue eyes. "Are you a good daddy?"

I shrug. "You'll have to give me a chance and let me know."

The gears in his head spin, and then he nods and returns to his drawing. "Okay."

Amelia and I share a look, one that requires a lot more discussion. Thankfully, the waitress returns with our food, giving Danny something else to focus on for a while.

We eat our meal in relative silence, but I love watching Danny dig into his food with gusto. He has a Scott appetite, one that I think Deacon will get a kick out of. "Hey bud, you're a good eater."

"He really is," Amelia agrees. "And he eats everything, including his vegetables."

Danny shoves a tater tot smothered in ketchup into his mouth, as if the compliment means he should act out.

Amelia tsks. "Ewww."

Danny giggles and grabs his napkin, cleaning his face. "I'm just kidding, Mommy."

She shakes her head but smiles, giving me a subtle tilt of her head. I love watching her in mommy mode. It's charming and awe-inspiring and it makes me want to do something to impress her.

After paying the waitress, we walk together to the parking lot. I stand outside her older sedan, already deciding she needs an SUV with the ultimate crash rating—nothing but the best for my son—and watch as she straps him into his car seat.

"Any suggestions on car seat brands?" I ask.

She nods. "He's five, so this is a booster seat. And yes, I can send you a few links tonight."

"When will I see you again?" Danny asks as Amelia steps away.

"Well, bud, your mom and I need to discuss that. When would you like to see me again?"

"Tomorrow!"

I glance at Amelia, and she nods. "Tomorrow it is."

Considering it's Saturday, I text Amelia to request she and Danny hang out at my place with Shaggy for dinner and a movie, since I have a game in the morning.

I always lie low the day before a game, whether it's on the road in a hotel room or at home.

Last night, I asked Phil—Deacon's personal assistant who I often call on—to buy me a dozen of the hottest toys out on the market for a five-year-old, so when Amelia and Danny arrive at my condo, I have my spare bedroom outfitted as a pseudo-playroom. I want him to know he has a room away from home until I can get a better place with a yard. I feel like my days of living in my condo, the consummate bachelor pad, are over. Danny deserves a big yard with a jungle gym and maybe even a pool.

I've been texting with Amelia all day. Not only about Danny, but about herself. She gave up her dreams when she found out she was pregnant, and I want to do what I can to repay her. She doesn't know it yet, but I put an order in for a Mercedes SUV, ranked best in class for safety. They need something better than what she is currently driving. I ordered myself one as well, because putting a car seat in a two-seater sports car isn't safe or legal.

I've also convinced her to bring Danny to the game tomorrow, confident my mom and sister will make her, her mother and brother feel welcome. London, Deacon's fiancée, will also be there, which will be a nice buffer for Amelia should my sister or mother get intense.

I know they are super excited to meet Danny and the woman who birthed their grandson/nephew.

We're sitting on the couch watching a Pixar movie with Danny laid out between us, a blanket draped over his little body. He's using my thigh as a pillow with his feet tucked up underneath his mom's back. Without thinking about it, I stretch my arm out across the back of the couch, my hand brushing Amelia's shoulder. Absent-mindedly, I play with her hair, not realizing it until she turns her head and looks at me, her eyebrow cocked in question.

I grin and pull my hand away. "Sorry."

She glances down at Danny, who is asleep on my thigh and then back up at me. "Are you ready for the game tomorrow?"

I shrug. "Sure. It should be one of our easier games of the season, so I'm not worried."

I finger a lock of hair hanging near her face, seemingly unable to keep my hands to myself. It's silky and smooth and reminds me of the two sexy mornings I stood chest-to-chest with her in the shower and washed her hair, or the hot nights when I fisted a handful as I pounded into her hot, wet pussy from behind.

"You know, if you and Danny want to stay the night, that room is yours."

She glances at the hallway leading to my spare bedroom and bites her lip. "I don't think that's a good idea."

"Why not?"

Sighing, she pulls her hair from my hand. "We have to be very intentional with our interactions, so as not to confuse Danny any more than necessary."

I frown. "What's there to confuse?"

"He might eventually wonder why his mommy and daddy aren't together."

"I'm wondering that, too."

She shakes her head and smiles. "Be serious, Declan."

"I am." It's so hard to have a conversation like this while whispering. "You were so terrified of having it look like you *trapped* me in a relationship that you ran and hid from me. I'm not saying starting something between us this way is ideal, but a child we love is a pretty damn good reason to try. It's definitely the best reason I've ever thought of."

I maneuver Danny so he's straddling my chest and then stand, carrying him into the spare bedroom. Amelia squeaks behind me, jumping up off the couch to follow us. Danny is a sound sleeper and snuggles in tighter against my chest. My heart swells under the cuteness and I wonder if this is what true unconditional love feels like.

If so, it's like heroin. No better rush in the world.

Laying him down, I cocoon Danny with a couple of the new plush animals and pull the blanket up over him. Amelia leans against the doorframe with her arms crossed over her chest, a sweet smile on her face. Looking at her as she watches me approvingly with our son, I'm more convinced than ever that she and I should have been a thing all those years ago.

We should have done this together.

And although I already know all her objections—Danny's welfare needs will be our number one concern—I also know she's just as attracted to me as I am to her, especially now that she's seen me with him.

I stand in front of her, looking down into her dark eyes and then gently take her hand and lead her out of the room. Without uttering a word, I take her into the living room, muting the Pixar animation so we can hear Danny if he wakes. I sit down and pull her into my lap, my eyes never leaving hers.

She shakes her head yet leans her body into my chest. "We shouldn't." Her voice is meek and holds no heat.

I stroke her hair and lean forward, kissing the tip of her nose. "I understand what you're thinking, but I'm positive you're wrong. Maybe we don't flaunt our relationship until we know where this is going, but we should definitely explore each other and what's between us." I grin, wicked thoughts dancing through my mind and registering on my face. "Especially each other."

Chapter Eight
Amelia

Football Sunday.

Declan made sure we have everything we need, including a car to pick us up at the house. They drive us into the players' parking lot and directly to the family and team elevator, where we bypass all the lines. Danny is beside himself, his energy matched only by my brother—both boys decked out in Rangers gear.

Hell, even my mom and I are wearing Declan's jerseys.

Waiting outside of the elevator are two women who could be none other than Linda and Deidre Scott—both blonde, beautiful, and statuesque.

"Well, I guess we know where Danny got his looks," my mom chirps.

I laugh as the driver opens the door. When Linda's gaze lands on Danny, a lone tear slips from her eye, and I can tell she's doing her best to keep her cool. Danny must sense their excitement, because my normally enthusiastic little boy grabs my hand and stands behind my leg, peeking out at them.

"Come on, Danny. Let's meet your daddy's family."

Danny grabs my mother's hand, and we walk forward as a trio.

Linda chokes back a sob. "Hello."

I smile. "Hi, Mrs. Scott."

She shakes her head. "No, no. Call me Linda."

"I'm Deirdre," a beautiful blonde with green eyes extends her hand.

"I'm Amelia and this is my mom, Vivian Pruitt. This is my brother Andrew and this little guy is Danny."

Deidre and Linda nod to everyone as they both bend over, Deidre dropping into a squat so she can get her near-six-foot-tall frame eye level. "Hi."

Danny ducks behind my leg and I tsk. "Since when are you shy?"

He brings his bright blue eyes up to mine and then straightens. "I'm not."

I chuckle and bring our joined hands forward to Linda. "Remember how we talked about how my mom is your grandma? Well, this is Declan's mom, your other grandma."

"I have two?"

I glance at my mom, worried this is breaking her heart. She was prepared to be Danny's everything for the rest of her life. To my utter amazement, my mother has a huge smile on her face as she nods to Danny and Linda. "You sure do, baby."

Linda pulls a frame out of her bag. "I have something to show you."

She hands it to Danny, who stares down at a picture that could be of him from twenty years ago.

"This is your daddy when he was your age." She glances up at me. "I can't believe how much they look alike."

He holds the picture up to me. "Look, Mommy. He looks like me."

"Very much so."

Deidre pipes in. "I'm your aunt."

He looks at her for a moment and then says, "I've never had an aunt before."

She giggles. "Well, good. Then I don't have any competition being the best aunt ever."

Linda straightens and motions to the elevator. "Should we go up? The game will start soon."

I nod and the six of us enter the elevator held by security. Once we're in, Linda mentions, "London, Deacon's fiancée, and the boys are already up there."

"Boys?"

"Three teenagers from London's apartment building that my son Deacon has taken under his wing. They are good boys, if not a little rough around the edges."

"But totally safe." Deidre nods to reassure me.

In the box, I'm introduced to London, Jo-Joe, Playboy and David.

London is a pretty woman with a dark edge. I already knew about her because of the articles written following Deacon's engagement announcement. They have kept speculation about her to a minimum and something tells me that's Deidre's doing. I know she's in charge of public relations and communication about the family because she's the one who schedules the post-game press conferences.

After we make introductions, I'm pleasantly surprised as the three teenage boys who look near grown welcome Andrew into their circle, showing him all the cool toys in the room. My mom and Linda migrate to a sofa with Danny on the floor between them playing with a bucket of blocks. My mom looks relaxed as she pulls out her phone and shows Linda five years' worth of photos—something I'm sure Declan's mom begrudges as well as appreciates.

This is harder than I thought it would be. My heart is full right now. I'm thankful Danny is surrounded by the love he deserves, but also troubled over my decisions to keep this from him. Declan's words come back to me. *"Five years I'll never get back."*

Deidre grabs a seltzer water and hands it to London. "Do you want something to drink?"

"The same, thanks." I motion to the giant engagement ring on London's hand and smile. "So, when's the big day?"

London gulps back her mouthful and then shrugs. "After the season, this spring."

"February sixteenth," Deidre adds.

I furrow my brow at London. "Do you not know your wedding date?"

"I do, it's just—"

"You're the press," Deidre finishes for her.

"What do you mean?"

Danny runs up to my leg at the same time that Andrew jumps into our conversation. He's never been great at social cues. "Can me and the guys take Danny down to the mezzanine to see the vendors?"

"Uh." I glance between the three boys and my brother. "I don't know, Andrew. There's got to be a million people down there to get lost in."

London leans in and whispers for me only to hear. "I trust these guys with my life. They won't let anything happen to them."

"Actually, I was hoping these young men would escort Vivian and me downstairs. I'd like to take them to the pro shop and show them our special edition jerseys." Linda gives me a reassuring nod. My mom follows it up with a subtle smile and I know it will be okay.

"We can do that," one boy, I think Playboy, says.

"Okay." I lean down and give Danny a kiss. "I love you. Don't run off."

"I won't."

As soon as they leave, I feel the tension in the room ratchet up to near uncomfortable levels. Deidre motions to the sofa, and we sit in a room with a giant glass wall separating us from seventy thousand screaming fans. The sheer magnitude of the crowd is overwhelming, their chatter near deafening levels and that's with an almost soundproof wall between us.

What will they sound like when Declan throws one of what I suspect will be four touchdowns this afternoon?

"What do you mean, I'm the press?" I turn back to Deidre, feeling like we need to get this out in the open.

"Well, Amelia. You're being welcomed into the Scott family inner circle and with that comes an expected amount of discretion. Your press badge has to be left out at the door."

"You know I'm no longer covering Rangers football. I was a temporary replacement for Mike."

"I know, but which column you write for isn't our concern, unless it's the gossip column. To be honest, Deacon's shotgun engagement won't make the back pages once we introduce Declan's child to the world."

A lead ball drops in my stomach. Is she threatening or warning me? "What do you mean?"

Deidre smiles. "Amelia, you are a journalist. How do you think they're going to write up Declan's five-year-old son? They are going to shred him as an absentee father."

"But that's not true."

She looks at me like I'm crazy. "Truth?"

I wave her away. "I know. As soon as it came out of my mouth, I heard it. To be fair, I haven't been a journalist for very long and I've never been interested in headline fodder."

"Well, luckily I have a few weeks head start, so when we break the story, I'll have everything in place and the chatter will not last more than a week or two."

"What if I came forward—"

Deidre shakes her head. "It won't matter. Anyone who wants to vilify Declan will use this to do so. Besides, he's adamant we don't discuss who, what, where, or why.

He said and I quote, *It's none of their fucking business why I'm only telling them about Danny and Amelia now,* end quote." She chuckles and shrugs. "He trusts me to take care of this and I will."

I bury my face in my hands and scream. When I was a scared and pregnant twenty-one-year-old, I didn't think about the ramifications this unveiling would hold. I never meant to hurt Declan, but only wanted to protect Danny and me.

The cushion next to me shifts and Deidre is wrapping her arm around my shoulder. "It's going to be fine. I promise."

"I never meant to hurt him. It was a crazy sex-filled weekend and nothing more."

"Nothing more?" London asks.

"Not for him."

"And you thought it was nothing more because he had the slut reputation," Deidre states versus asks with a knowing smile on her face.

I shrug, not denying her observation. "People are going to hate him for something that isn't his fault."

Deidre leans back into the sofa. "I'll tell you the most positive and negative personality trait both my brothers have in abundance—neither one of them gives a shit what the public at large thinks of them. I don't know if it's a star football player thing that gives them such unshakeable confidence, but Deacon and Declan are so infuriatingly sure of themselves that no one else's opinion matters. Except Danny's. I think Declan cares what Danny thinks of him."

Last night, as Declan and I made out on the couch for an hour, he told me something similar, except he said my opinion matters to him, too. He wants to date me, understanding I want to hide our relationship from Danny until we know how serious we are. He says he's already serious, although I can't see how that can be true after two afternoons.

I fell for him that weekend, never thinking I was more than another conquest for his books.

How do you date the father of your child? This entire thing is as back-ass-ward as you can get. What's the old rhyme? *First came love, then came marriage, then came a baby in a baby carriage.* Well, we certainly screwed that up.

"Game is starting," London says, getting up and opening the sliding glass door to the outside patio overlooking the field, letting the veritable force of the energy from the fans below blast into the room.

At the same time, Danny comes rushing into the room with the rest of his entourage in tow, his arms wrapped around a giant plush mascot. "Did I miss kickoff?"

"No. You want to sit outside and watch from the railing?"

"Yes!"

"Okay, but no climbing and no throwing anything over. You got me?"

"Yes, Mommy."

Andrew and his new friends go outside with Danny,

and I know they will take care of him by the way they put him in the middle of their group.

London smiles and nods her head as if she can read my thoughts. "David has a brother who is on the spectrum, so they're used to hanging out with someone like Andrew."

"Andrew isn't on the spectrum. A car hit him on his twelfth birthday, and he suffered a TBI. He has APD—Arrested Psychological Development. Pretty much, his development stopped at twelve, even though his body keeps aging. Luckily, he was a pretty mature twelve-year-old, so mostly, he can function on his own. He stays close to help our mother and vice versa. But I've noticed these guys are pretty great. I appreciate them including him. Most people are leery of Andrew until they get to know him."

"Yeah, no... not these guys. They're great." London stares out the window at them and smiles. "So, I hope Deidre didn't scare you or anything. She's great at her job and protective of the family."

"She didn't scare me, but she made a point I hadn't really considered before. Declan doesn't deserve a bunch of hate. He's only known for a couple of days and his reaction to Danny has been better than I've ever dreamed possible. Nothing about his public presence off the field led me to believe he'd take to becoming a dad so easily. It really makes me regret not coming to him sooner."

"I don't know Declan very well. Actually, I don't know any of the Scotts very well. Deacon and I only reconnected a few months ago and our relationship wasn't real at first." London looks over her shoulder and says the last part quietly, almost under her breath.

"What?" I also drop my voice and my head toward hers.

"It's a long story we can discuss at a later time, but now the wedding is real. The love is real." She blushes and I'm betting she's thinking about her private time with Deacon. "Everything between us is very real."

"Ah, so Declan's bedroom skills are a family gift." I chuckle, my blush matching hers.

"Have you?" London's eyes grow wide as she clutches my forearm.

It takes me half a second to realize what she's asking. "No. No. Not..." *Yet* is on the tip of my tongue. I know it's going to happen, even if my brain tells me getting romantically involved with Declan is a bad idea. Our make-out session last night reminds me of the passion we shared, my lady bits tingling as he woke them out of a long, hard slumber. And he never even touched me below the belt. How he did that with just his lips and tongue, I can't explain, but one kiss from Declan Scott and every comatose nerve in my body roared to life.

"Like I said, I don't know Declan very well, but he's been super nice and supportive of me from day one. Deacon announced our engagement to his family, much like he announced it to the world... a complete and utter mic drop moment. But Declan's always been welcoming."

"He is nice." I glance up at the television screen, which is zeroed in on the man as he deliberates with the offensive coordinator. He's beyond beautiful, his dark blond hair matted and sweaty around his forehead. I've been watching him for years, refusing to let my mind run away with fantasies I thought were too absurd to come true.

After last night, I'm wondering if I should let my imagination run wild and envision a future where Declan, Danny and I are a family?

One thing is for certain, I'm definitely going to let Declan kiss me again.

Chapter Nine
Declan

"Another amazing game. Did you hear Seattle lost today? That puts the Rangers back as number one in the league." I nod and smile, but say nothing, considering they've asked me no questions. I usually love after-game press conferences, but all I really want to do is join my family upstairs.

My family. Fucking surreal.

Amelia wants us to go slow, which I admit, goes against my nature. I've never tiptoed into anything a day in my life, which includes being the fastest childbirth my mom ever had. She barely made it to the hospital before I entered the world, which makes me wonder what Amelia went through with Danny.

We have so much history to catch up on.

We take a couple more questions, but even the reporters can tell that my heart's not in it. Yes, we had an amazing game. Yes, we blew out our competition. No, I don't feel like gloating about it, which is definitely not textbook Declan.

Ten minutes later, Deacon, my father and I enter the elevator and ride it up to the family suite, a room I haven't been to in years. All heads swing our way as we open the door, but it's a gleeful *Daddy* being shouted across the room that causes my heart to clench and the world to stop spinning. I look down in time to see Danny running full speed toward me. Without thinking, I push Deacon out of the way so I can swoop my little boy up into my arms.

"You won!"

"We sure did. Did you see the touchdown I ran in myself?"

"Yeah!"

"That one was for you, bud."

Deacon walks up with his arm around London's shoulder. "Introduce me."

I chuckle and poke Deacon in the chest. "Danny, this is my big brother, Deacon. He's your uncle, like Andrew is your uncle."

"I know, Daddy. Auntie Deidre already told me all about him." Danny smiles at Deacon.

"Auntie, huh?" I glance at my sister as she walks toward us with a huge smile on her face. "Oh yeah, I got that sh... stuff on lock."

I shake my head at her, realizing we're all going to have to watch our language around young, impression-able ears.

My mom then walks up with my dad. "Danny, this is your grandpa." She smiles at me and explains, "He asked if he was going to have a papa, because he doesn't have one at his house."

My dad smiles down at him and offers him his hand. They do a little awkward shake. "It's nice to meet you, little Declan."

I look around the room to find Amelia and her mother Vivian watching us from afar—gifting the Scott family with this moment—and throw her a wink. She smiles, a slight blush darkening her cheeks.

Danny kicks his legs—something I've quickly learned is a small child's universal signal to put them down. He runs across the room and grabs a picture frame and holds it above his head. "Look Daddy, we look the same."

"Two good-looking guys, right?" I cross the room and slide next to Amelia, purposefully wrapping my arm around her waist and pressing a kiss to her neck. She stiffens, but I pretend to ignore it. Then I lean in front of her and meet Vivian's eyes. "Hi again."

She smiles and chuckles softly. Last time we met, Amelia asked me not to tell her what I knew was true in my heart, but the looks Vivian gave me let me know she suspected something. Amelia confirmed that for me during our talk last night.

Speaking of our talk last night. "Could I have a couple of minutes with you in private?"

Amelia nods and shares a look with her mother that speaks volumes.

Watch Danny.

Keep everyone distracted.

We'll be right back.

I grab her hand and pull her into the en-suite bathroom, the only place to grab a few minutes of privacy. The door barely latches shut before I have her back pressed against the door, my lips on hers. She sinks into me, running her hands up my arms and into my hair as I lift her legs, coaxing her into wrapping them around my waist. Our tongues tangle with each other, my body roaring to life despite my exhaustion.

Pulling back to break our kiss, I smile down at her. "I missed you."

"You did?"

"Yeah. Even though you left early last night so I could get a good night's sleep, all I did was toss and turn, thinking about how badly I need you in my bed. I'm desperate to touch you, taste you, explore every inch of you again."

She giggles. "I did the same. Your kisses definitely woke something in me that has been dormant for a long time."

"Stay with me tonight."

Shaking her head, she pushes gently against my chest, forcing me to let her down. "I can't. Danny has school tomorrow. I have to get him home, bathed and in bed at a reasonable hour or he's going to be a nightmare in the morning."

"When can I see you again?"

"I don't know. We have a routine during the week that I'm not sure how to interrupt."

I swipe a chunk of hair behind her ear and tilt her chin up so she's looking at me. "I have out-of-town games next weekend and the weekend after that. For the next three months, I'll be traveling every other weekend or more and I can't wait until the end of the season for our first date. What do you normally do with Danny when you have a date?"

She bites her lip, her eyes darting past me to look at the wall or the mirror or whatever—anything other than my eye. "I haven't had a date since I had Danny, so I can't tell you what a night away from him is like."

Her words suck all the air out of my lungs. "Not one date?"

She shakes her head.

"Holy shit, Amelia. We have to figure this out, because if I had my way, we'd move you and Danny in today and I'd have you underneath me tonight."

"Oh Declan. That's your hormones talking."

I brazenly grab her hand and put it against my aching cock. "Yes and no, Amelia. I've been chasing the feeling I had with you that weekend for years. Nothing has compared to what we shared, but I didn't know it until I saw you in the press room a few weeks ago. One look at you and all the memories came rushing back, and then I realized it's been you I've been searching for the whole time."

She flexes her fingers, kneading me through my jeans, and I groan. "Maybe you should give me and Danny a ride home and tuck him and then me into bed tonight."

I grin. "I can do that."

After giving Danny a bath, I run into Vivian as I go into the kitchen to grab him a half cup of water for his bedside while Amelia dresses him in his pajamas.

"Today was nice. I'm thrilled Danny will have a big family to enjoy. Your mother is lovely," she says with a small smile on her lips but keeps her gaze on her cup of tea.

Leaning my hips against the counter, I face her and wait until she lifts her gaze to meet mine. "I'm really sorry I wasn't there for Amelia and Danny and, honestly, you. I can never express my gratitude to you for taking care of them all these years."

She places her fingers gently on my forearm. "There's really nothing to apologize for, Declan. You didn't know. But you're here now and that's all that matters."

"I'm going to marry your daughter," I state with absolute authority. Although I sound crazy, I've never been more sure of anything in my life. "She doesn't know it yet, but I feel it deep within my soul. If I had been more mature when we met, maybe things would have been different. All I can do now is try to create the perfect future for us."

"It doesn't have to be perfect, Declan, just authentic. Lead with your heart and the rest will fall into place." She stares at me with her dark brown eyes so similar to Amelia's.

Danny comes running into the kitchen with Amelia following behind him. "Night Nana."

Vivian bends down and wraps her arms around Danny. "Good night, my precious boy."

When she lets him go, he turns and grabs my hand. "Come on, Daddy. Time for bed."

I chuckle and meet Vivian's eyes again. "Thank you." She nods.

"What was that about?" Amelia asks when we get into Danny's room.

"I'll tell you later."

"I want Daddy to read to me tonight. Is that okay, Mommy?"

Amelia smiles and nods, pulling the covers up to his shoulders before turning and handing me a book. "Start on page six."

For the next ten minutes, I read from The Turtle's Dove, holding it in one hand while slowly reaching across the bed to interlace my fingers with Amelia's. Danny takes no time to pass out, the excitement of the day wearing him out. We walk hand in hand into the kitchen, where Vivian flashes us a small smile.

Amelia tries to pull her hand out of mine, but I'm not having it and hold her tight.

"I'm taking my tea and my book and heading to bed." Vivian makes a show of grabbing her reading glasses and her mug. "I made you a sandwich, Declan, in case you're hungry. Good night and I'll see you in the morning."

I wait until her bedroom door closes before I grin

down at Amelia. "I think your mom just low-key gave me permission to spend the night."

"It certainly sounds that way." Amelia grabs the plate she left behind and pulls me into the living room. "Would you like something to drink?"

I put the sandwich aside and pull her into my arms before she can protest, locking lips in a possessive kiss that makes her melt into me. Sitting down, I pull her onto my lap, caging her with my arms as she gives herself over, her tongue dancing with mine. Last night, we made out like a couple of teenagers—clothes on, lips swollen, my fingers tracing the lines of her nipples buried under her T-shirt and bra. While I'm willing to take all the time she needs until she's ready to take me into her bed, like a teenage boy, I'm going to test and tease her limits every chance I get.

I slide my hand in between her jean-clad thighs, encouraged when she spreads them a little wider. Fuck, memories of our weekend together have haunted me for weeks. It took everything within me not to approach her after that first press conference, not knowing what I know now. I can't believe that was only six weeks ago.

Last month, I was a bachelor intent on scoring a few nights with a chick who I shared an amazing weekend with during my senior year in college.

Now, I'm the father of a five-year-old, hoping to convince his mom to give me a chance and one day become my wife.

"Maybe we should take this to my bedroom, just in case Andrew comes into the house."

I stand up without saying a word, cradling her in my arms like a new bride. "Just tell me where to go."

"Bedroom to the left of Danny's."

Carrying her into her room, I lay her down on the bed and then gently close the door, silently kicking off my shoes. Is this what married sex is like? I suppose so—stolen moments trying to be as quiet as possible so as not to alert curious ears.

She stifles a giggle by slapping her hand over her mouth as I rush to pull off my shirt, also flinging it to the floor. I sprawl out next to her on the bed, propping my head on my hand as I rest my other on her hip. We stare at each other for several seconds in silence and then she attacks, rolling me to my back.

Amelia straddles my waist and kisses me hard. I slide my hands up her sides and under her shirt, the heat of her flesh warming my fingers. She does me one better, lifting and pulling off her top and bra.

My breath rushes out as I get my first look at her, the same but better than the girl I knew so many years ago. Her breasts are fuller, heavy as I cup them in my hands and infinitely sexy.

She closes her eyes and drops her head back, moaning lowly. "It's been forever since someone touched me."

"I'm really sorry about that. I'm going to do everything I can to make it up to you."

I unbuckle her jeans and roll her onto her back, sliding them down her legs. "Tonight is about your pleasure. We'll go as far as you want. Just let me take care of you."

She runs her fingers over the muscles in my back as I press my body down on hers. "Whenever I take care of myself, I always fantasize about you and that weekend."

"Sounds like I owe you six years' worth of orgasms."

"Then you better get started." She grins.

Now that is a challenge I'm up for.

Chapter Ten
Amelia

One thing I vividly remember about my weekend with Declan is his talent for being everywhere at the same time. While he's trailing kisses down my neck and lavishing my nipple with his tongue, his hands are sliding down my body, fingers digging into the backs of my thighs. His brand of lovemaking is all-consuming, every nerve ending lighting up under his masterful touch.

"Don't be offended if I'm quiet. I've learned to keep the noise coming out of my bedroom to a minimum so curious minds don't come barging in."

Declan chuckles as he moves lower down my body, kissing my soft midsection. "I won't take it personally, although it gives me more incentive to whisk you away for a weekend where you can scream your pleasure."

He spreads my legs apart, using his finger to trace the opening to my pussy. Holding the glistening digit up, he throws me that cocky smile he often uses on the press. "One thing I remember about you is how responsive you are to my touch. I love how wet you get for me. You fit me so perfectly. I never should've let you slip away, but now that you're mine, I have no intentions of letting you go."

Although he keeps his eyes on mine, he lowers his mouth, running his tongue along my slit while hoisting my thighs up on his shoulders, pushing my legs apart. The first touch of his tongue against my clit sends a tingle up my spine, my nipples puckering with desire. I moan softly, grabbing a throw pillow to muffle my impending cries of ecstasy. Sure, by myself, with the quietest clit vibrator money can buy, I've learned to bite my lip as I self-pleasure, but having Declan between my legs is a different ballgame and I don't think I can keep the passion from erupting out of my mouth.

When he latches onto my clit, alternating between a biting and sucking motion, I'm lost, tossing my head back and forth as I cry out my release into the pillow.

He growls. "That's my girl. Give me every drop of sweet cream you have."

My thighs clamp down around his head, but he knows how to coax every bit out of me. He intuitively knew it the moment we met, saying all the right words, touching me gently and then more firmly in all the right ways. Declan Scott knew my body before he knew my mind, and he had no problem burrowing his way into my heart.

But it wasn't all sex that weekend.

Don't get me wrong—there was a lot of sex—but we also talked about our dreams and the future. I knew what he wanted, his sole focus to be the number one quarterback in the league, breaking records and setting all-time highs. He knew I wanted to be a reporter, working alongside one of the best in the state. He had multiple teams courting him with his family's team as a backup. I had my internship immediately following graduation.

We didn't talk much about who we were before that weekend.

For example, I never told him about my father dying that summer and my stress about coming home to an irrevocably changed house that Christmas. Nor did I tell him about my brother, or that we were from the same town. Declan is part of the north side elite, richer than all of Starlite Park combined. I'm from the west side, which is full of old-town charm, much of which is weathered and aged. I guess if he had known we were from the same town, he might have looked and found Danny and me earlier.

Another thing I have to regret.

Declan leaves a trail of kisses up my body as he rests beside me, pulling my thigh up over his soft nylon joggers. "That's one of about eighteen hundred orgasms I owe you."

I chuckle, tossing the pillow aside to look at him. "Where are you getting that number?"

"Six years times approximately three hundred orgasms a year, give or take a couple hundred."

I arch my brow. "Give or take? In our first weekend together, you gave me at least a dozen orgasms. So, I'd say you're shooting a little low."

"Ouch." He grins, brushing back the hair from my

face to stroke my cheek. "You forget, I'm out of town at least four days a month for about four months a year."

I shake my head. "That's sixteen times six. Try again."

"Okay, okay. So that was one of about three thousand orgasms."

Chuckling, I run my hand up his bicep and over his broad shoulder to cup his jaw. "You've accumulated quite the debt."

"I'm willing to work it off any way you want." He leans forward and kisses my lips sweetly, pulling me with him as he rolls to his back.

Sighing, I lay my head on his chest and let my fingers explore the ridges of his eight-pack. "I owe you, too. So maybe we're even?"

"Different debts. Besides, I like the idea of owing you and you owing me. It'll keep us mindful of what we're building here."

"Are we building something?" I lift my head and look him in the eye.

"You and me and a baby makes three, right?"

Shaking my head, I smile. "I was thinking of that nursery rhyme the other day."

"I know this seems fast, but honestly, this is six years in the making. I'm all in, Amelia. If you're not sure about me, then I'll take the time you need for me to convince you, but I already know what I want. I want you, me and Danny together, as a family—living, playing, and growing with each other."

I return my head to his chest, his words bouncing

around in my head. Can he really mean it? Us, together as a family?

It's too much to ponder right now. Instead, I let my fingers do the walking, letting him know what's on my mind as I slide my hand under his joggers and grip the massive erection I remember fondly.

Declan hisses, his abdominal muscles tightening. "What are you doing, Amelia?"

"I'm exploring. Isn't that what you said we should do?"

"Yes," he groans as I pull him free of his joggers and stroke his impressive length. "But I thought you wanted to go slow."

"I never said we had to go slow." Sliding down his body, I put my mouth near the head of his cock that is glistening with pre-cum. "I said we had to hide from Danny until we were sure where this was going."

"Are you sure?"

I lick my lips and meet his eyes. "Let's talk in the morning."

He nods, his bright blue eyes shining as I open my mouth and stick out my tongue, purposefully maintaining eye contact as I slowly wrap my lips around the tip.

Declan closes his eyes, his chest rising and falling with labored breaths as I take him deep within my mouth. He groans, his hand fisting the bedspread next to his hip as I work him with my tongue and tease him with my teeth.

"Fuck, Amelia. That feels good."

Popping him free from my lips, I kiss the tip and look

up into his eyes. I can't believe I'm about to ask this, but I feel like if he meant everything he said earlier, then this is the most appropriate thing I can say to tell him how I'm feeling. "Will you make love to me, Declan?"

A slow smile takes over his face. He pulls me up to claim my lips. "Every night for the rest of my life, Amelia."

Declan rolls me to my back and then stands, pulling off his joggers.

"Maybe we should get under the covers?" I suggest, my mind racing to all the people on the other side of my bedroom door.

"Should I lock the door?" Declan arches his brow.

I bite my lip and ponder. I've never locked my son out of my room before, but then again, I've never had a reason to. "Maybe?"

"Let's get under the covers. I don't want you distracted by what lurks beyond these walls." Declan turns off the overhead light and then slides under the covers with me, the two of us blanketed in darkness and cocooned in warmth.

Our visual exploration is over. Now we're guided by simple touch that feels anything but simple. He settles his weight between my legs, the heaviness of his hard cock lying against my thigh. "Are you sure about this?"

I frame his face with my hands and gently kiss his lips. "Yes."

Declan kisses me breathless while this little room— my childhood bedroom—becomes our entire world. Gripping my thigh, he slides his hand down until he's cupping my knee and pulling me wide, the tip of his cock pushing against my slick entrance.

On instinct, I arch my back, lifting my hips into the air, silently begging him to slide forward. He doesn't waste time teasing me, gliding his hard cock into my wet channel inch by glorious inch.

He groans, burying his mouth into my neck. "Fuck, you are so tight."

"Kegels, baby." I moan softly, arching up and wrapping my legs around his waist. He adjusts the blankets to keep us covered and then works himself in and out of me with smooth, deep strokes.

"Oh god!" I moan a little louder than expected.

He chuckles and seals his lips over mine to swallow the sound, all while turning me into a sopping wet mess with each thrust of his hips. It takes no time to bring me to the edge again, Declan's cock perfectly curved to stroke my g-spot.

My legs shake as my pussy clamps down, gripping and milking his cock with my climax. I whimper and moan, clutching at his shoulders as he slows his pace, allowing me to catch my breath. "Fuck, woman. You feel even better than I remember."

Panting, I lick my lips and meet his bright blue eyes. "You're amazing."

"No, we're amazing... together."

Chapter Eleven
Declan

I wake up to movement on the bed, a four-foot-tall boy with bright blue eyes staring down at me. Instinct tells me to remain calm and act like this is no big deal.

Spook in front of a child and they get spooked. Freak out and hover over a kid who fell and skinned their knee, and they will scream bloody murder, but give them a cool, *this isn't a big deal, lets clean you up* pep talk and they calm down to match your energy.

So, I flash him a small smile and say softly, "Good morning, Champ."

"Why are you sleeping in Mommy's bed?"

I glance at Amelia who is lying still but has her eyes open, watching the situation unfold, concern darkening her gaze.

"Well, your mommy and I stayed up late talking, and I was too tired after playing football to drive home. Is that okay?"

He shrugs and lies down between us. "I guess so. Will you take me to school today?"

I glance at my watch, thankful Amelia and I put on our clothes before we fell asleep. I wasn't supposed to stay the night. After we got dressed, I climbed back into bed with her, telling her I'd hold her for a bit before taking off. Of course, sexually sated and exhausted from my day, I promptly fell asleep.

"It's only four. Why are you up so early?"

"I can't wait to tell Bobby and Cindy and Rittzi about the game. I'm going to show off my jersey."

"Danny, baby. We have two more hours to sleep," Amelia says, reaching out to stroke his cheek.

"Can I sleep with you?"

I snake my arm around his waist and pull him into my chest, but I lock my eyes with Amelia's. She smiles, but there are tears filling her eyes—tears of joy, I hope.

"I love you," I mouth over Danny's head.

She blinks and then nods almost imperceptibly, finally mouthing back to me. "I love you, too."

Even though I know it's going to take time, this feels like an important step in the right direction.

A few hours later, I'm driving with Amelia to Danny's school. He insists I walk him to class, where we disrupt a classroom of thirty kids and a very excited teacher who is a Rangers fan. I answer a dozen questions before Amelia and I duck out of there.

"Can you skip work today?" I bring our joined hands up to my lips and kiss her fingers.

"Can you?"

"Yeah, we usually get a down day after a game."

"And how would you like to spend the day?" She grins, letting me pull her tight against my body.

"We could spend it in bed." I lean my head forward and kiss her neck. "Or we could cruise some neighborhoods and look at houses for sale."

"What?"

"We don't have to move in together today, but I think you and Danny don't want to live in a high-rise condo, so we need to figure out which neighborhoods we want to live in."

She shakes her head. "You're crazy."

"Why? Because I know what I want and I don't want to wait?"

"Because you believe you know what you want. What if you change your mind in three months?"

"I won't." I cradle her face with my hands, making sure her eyes look nowhere but into mine.

"I want to believe you, Declan." Her eyes fill with unshed tears. "I really do. But it's too crazy to comprehend."

"What will it take for you to believe me?" I kiss her cheek, the tip of her nose and then her lips. "Would you believe me if you were my wife?"

She sucks in her breath and stares at me. "What?"

I grin. "You heard me, Amelia. Marry me. Be my wife. Tell me to put another baby inside you and let's grow our family."

Amelia slides her hands up my chest and wraps her hands around my neck. "I can't believe I'm saying this, but yes."

"Yes what?"

"Yes, Declan, I will marry you."

Epilogue
Amelia

The roar from the seventy-five thousand fans is deafening and even little Danny has his hands slapped over his ears as they lead us onto the field and up on the podium where they're presenting the Scott family with the championship trophy. As soon as Declan sees us, he swoops Danny into his arms and then pulls me to his side, kissing me with the passion we usually reserve for the bedroom.

"Declan!" A reporter steps right into our moment, yelling to be heard over the fans. "This has been quite the year for you. First your son and fiancée, now MVP and your first championship ring. You must be overwhelmed right now."

"Gratitude, man. That's all I'm feeling right now—like I'm the luckiest SOB ever."

"You have an amazing team supporting you—"

"On and off the field," Declan interjects.

The reporter chuckles. "Do you think you'll carry this momentum into next year?"

"This year was only the beginning. With my family and my teammates by my side, there's nothing we can't accomplish."

With those last words, Declan accepts the MVP trophy, raising it over his head before presenting it to Danny, who smiles big for the cameras. He's such a ham and probably destined to be a Rangers football player someday.

I mostly keep my head tucked into Declan's neck—uncomfortable with the limelight—although, I suppose I better get used to it considering I'll be working in team communications next season. Deidre asked me to use my journalism degree to help her wrangle the public relations team and manage the press conferences. I'm excited about the opportunity, and I think Deidre will teach me a lot. I just hope working for the family doesn't put a strain on my relationship with Declan.

Once the MVP presentation is done, we're shuffling to the back of the podium to let the mayhem continue. Declan lowers his mouth to my ear, partially so I can hear him, partially to tease me by nipping at my earlobe.

"I can't wait to get you to our suite. Mom and Dad are going to take Danny for the night. You and I are going to test the durability of every surface in that room, as well as the thickness of the walls."

I giggle and smack his chest. "Behave."

"Absolutely not. I'm going to put a baby in you tonight, Amelia, and wrap up the perfect season."

Pulling back, I give him a raise of my brow. I wasn't going to tell him until we were home, but now seems perfect. "Can you get a second baby in there when I'm already pregnant?"

"What?" Declan sets Danny down and frames my face with his hands. "Say that again."

"It's very early, but the stick I peed on three days ago says I'm pregnant."

Declan lowers his head to mine. "Oh, Amelia. This is the best day of my life."

The players head to the locker room to shower and change while the family heads to the hotel ballroom for a team celebration. Declan, Deacon and London taught me weeks ago who I should avoid—several players' wives showing next-level toxicity. The joke around the family is they are bucking for their own reality TV show, the *Housewives of the Rocky Mountain Rangers*, with Aggie's ex-wife leading the pack even though she is no longer part of the inner circle.

Speaking of Aggie, I noticed after the division championships that he and Deidre seemed to spend a lot of time chatting around the fireplace. I wonder what's going on there?

Declan comes into the room with most of the players, his eyes scanning the crowd to find me. We spend the next hour mingling before he takes me by the hand and leads me out of the party without a word of goodbye to anyone. Actually, I noticed Deacon and London did the same thing about fifteen minutes ago. Since Linda and my mom already took Danny to bed, I have no one else I have to say goodbye to—although I do catch Deidre and Aggie talking on the balcony as if they are the only two people in the world.

I'll have to ask her about that the next girls' brunch we have.

Within a matter of months, the Scott family has welcomed us into their inner circle, my mother and I finding camaraderie with a group of strong, educated, and powerful women. I think my mom found a friend in Linda that she didn't realize she needed, which makes my whirlwind romance with Declan easier.

Declan pulls me into his arms once the elevator doors close, burying his face into my neck and sighing.

"Are you okay?"

"Honestly, I feel like crying."

"What?" I wrap my arms around his back and rub his muscles. "What's wrong?"

He pulls back to pin me in place with his brilliant blue eyes. "I'm so fucking happy right now. You make me happy."

I smile. "And you make us happy."

He half-chuckles, half-snorts and shakes his head. "I didn't know what I was missing until you and Danny came into my life. A piece of me was missing, but now I feel full. I wish we could get married tomorrow, but I don't want to fuck with Deacon and London's day—plus my sister would kill us if we snuck off."

"Yeah, she would." I smile, rubbing my thumb over

the stubble on his chin. I can't wait to feel it between my legs, roughing up my skin, leaving me with a gentle burn I'll feel for days. "Now that the season is over, we have plenty of time to set up our new home, and I don't need a piece of paper to know I'm yours and you're mine."

"Damn right, you're mine." Declan tilts his head and rests his forehead against mine. "I love you so much."

"I love you, too."

Second Epilogue
Declan - Eight Months Later...

I sit in a chair in the room's corner with my face in my hands. Amelia is quiet for the moment, but every few minutes she either moans or outright screams in pain, and it's killing me to be utterly useless in this situation.

My mother-in-law, Vivian, placates me with a gentle rub of my shoulder. "This is normal."

"She's been in and out of it for fourteen hours. Was it like this with Danny?"

"No. Danny came quickly and without complaint. They say the second child is always a handful, although usually a shorter labor. However, Amelia's delivery was a lot harder on me than Andrew's, that's for sure—a lot more false labor with her than him. Why don't you take a break? Your family is eating breakfast in the other room."

We have a private suite at Memorial Hospital which includes a family room and separate patient space with a private bath, but I sent the family out for food because their hovering was grating on my last nerve.

I shake my head. "I'm not leaving her. I wasn't here last time, so I'm not missing a minute this time."

Vivian smiles down at me and then places a motherly kiss on my forehead. "Okay. Do you want something to eat or drink?"

"No. Thanks."

Amelia moans and turns her head, her eyes fluttering open. "You look worse than I feel."

I chuckle, grabbing her hand and bringing it to my lips. "Good, I guess."

"Have you slept at all?"

"Not really."

"You should lie down."

"Don't worry about me. What can I do for you?"

She takes a deep breath and rubs her belly. "Tell your little girl to get her butt in gear. She's late and pissing me off."

Throughout this pregnancy, Amelia has shown me how much stronger women are than men. In comparison, we are pansies—sniveling, whining, cry-babies who should thank god we aren't built to do what only the fairer sex can do. I don't think, no matter how many times and in what graphic detail we are told, that we can grasp the difference between the sexes until we love a woman and watch her go through ten months of pregnancy. Only then do we even slightly understand, and I know I will never be as tough as my beautiful wife is right now.

I stand up and lean forward, pressing my lips to her belly. "Hey little Belle, it's time to go. You have a large audience waiting for you out here, and this is next-level diva bull-shit, making everyone wait for you." Tears fall from my eyes and splash onto Amelia's stretched stomach while our child plays the drums inside her warm and cozy home. I don't think I've ever been more scared in my life than I am right now. At first, it was excitement as we rushed to the hospital. A couple of hours later, it turned into anxiousness. Now—fear.

I hate this.

I hate being helpless.

I hate watching the love of my life whimper in pain and be unable to do anything about it.

Amelia runs her fingers through my hair at the same time another contraction hits. Her fingers tense and then she pushes my head away, as if I need to get clear before she either hits me or pulls my hair out. I'd take either at the moment.

"I'm never touching you again," I say once her breathing is under control, taking a damp cloth to wipe her forehead.

"Yes, you will. Otherwise, I'll tackle you to the ground and run my tongue all over you until you give up the goods."

I chuckle. "Don't turn me on right now."

"How are we doing?" Our OBGYN walks in with scrubs on, which I'm hoping is a good sign. Regardless, the question raises my hackles, and the desire to punch the doctor for asking such a dumb question tells me all I need to know.

I'm tired, I'm on the edge, and I'm over this.

"Please tell me we're ready," Amelia half moans, half whines, as she squeezes my fingers.

"I hope so. I have a tee time at noon."

I raise my brow.

He looks at me and wipes the smile off his face. "I'm kidding. Jeez, rough room. Okay, okay, you're tired. Let's take a look."

The doctor positions Amelia's legs and then does the damn measuring thing he's been doing every hour for the last twelve. "Ten centimeters. We're ready."

"Oh, thank god," Amelia sighs.

For the next forty-five minutes, my wife goes through hell, but is gifted with a crying baby wrapped in a fuzzy pink blanket when it's all done. After the nursing and birthing center staff finish cleaning everything up, the grandparents come in with Danny leading the charge. "Can I see the baby?"

I pick up my son and rest him on my hip as we look down at Amelia and little Annabelle Daniella Scott.

"She's beautiful." My mom's voice cracks through her tears.

"She certainly is, son." My father nods and then places a soft hand over Amelia's. "How do you feel?"

Vivian stands at the end of the bed, rubbing her daughter's calves while Amelia flashes my father a sweet smile. "Tired, but happy."

"We should probably let you sleep." My mother wipes away her tears.

"Don't you want to hold your granddaughter before you leave?"

A sob escapes my mom's lips. I was the first one to hold my little girl, and I cut her cord—an experience that has no comparison—but the look on my mother's face right now is priceless. I lift my phone and take a picture of her. "Yes, please."

I switch to video and capture the moment my mother holds her second grandchild, but the first infant. Danny, who is probably exhausted even though I know he slept most of the night in the other room, rests his head on my shoulder and watches the exchange.

"Is there room for four more in here?" Deidre pokes her head in.

"The more the merrier," Amelia says through a yawn.

I'm giving them fifteen minutes, and then I'm kicking everyone out so my wife can sleep.

Deidre walks in with Aggie by her side, followed by Deacon and London, who is wearing a small baby bump of her own.

"Ohhh!" Deidre coos, pressing a soft kiss to the top of Annabelle's head. "She's so precious and smells so good. She's not gross at all, Deacon."

Deacon turns red-faced. "I said nothing of the sort, Buster."

London giggles beside him.

Deidre's grin widens, and she reaches out, running her fingers through Amelia's hair. "I'm sure you're ready to pass out. Is there anything we can get you before we go?"

"I have everything I need and more right here." She reaches out and squeezes my thigh.

I stop the video and slip my phone back into my pocket, setting Danny down next to Amelia on the bed. Then I reach out and grab Vivian's hand, pulling her to my side and pressing a kiss against her temple. "My heart is so full right now. I'm thankful to have all of you here."

"But now get out?" Deidre raises her eyebrow in a taunt.

"Just you."

She sticks her tongue out and Aggie shakes his head, slipping his arm around her waist and pulling her back against his chest. Our eyes lock for a second and I see pure happiness on my offensive lineman's face, something that is long overdue.

"I love you, Mommy," Danny says softly, as if to not be overheard.

She strokes his hair. "I love you too, baby."

"Can we go home now?" He looks back at me.

"Mommy, Annabelle, and I have to stay until tomorrow, but whenever you want to go home, Nana will take you. I'm sure you're exhausted." I rub his back.

"No. I'll stay here with you for now. Okay, Nana?"

Vivian nods.

My mom gives Annabelle back to Amelia, Danny staring at his baby sister with a gentle fascination that wraps a death grip around my heart. I stare lovingly down at my family in what is the best moment in my life —championship trophies be damned.

This is what's important, right here.

Six weeks later...

Once a week since bringing Annabelle, or Belle for short, home, Vivian stays at our place to give us what she calls a night of solid sleep. I can't believe she does it, but I'm not going to tell her no. I think after being so heavily involved with Danny's rearing, she's feeling a little left out this second time around. Of course, with me traveling to away games, she's staying over more often than not.

Again, I don't mind. I'll give that woman whatever she wants until the day she's gone.

My cock rouses before my mind fully wakes, the sunshine coming through our window alerting me to the hour. Then my brain engages and I realize it's not another erotic dream causing me to be hard, but Amelia's warm, wet lips working me from under the sheets.

"Ah, Amelia. What are you doing?" My voice is rough and ragged.

She works me harder, causing me to throw my head back as I slide my fingers into her silky hair.

"Amelia, baby, stop," I pant, close to losing control.

She pops me free of her mouth, her hand continuing to move up and down in slow, languid strokes. I pull the sheets off her head to look down at her, her eyes hooded with desire. "Good morning."

"I guess." I wrap my fingers around her arms and pull her up my body, claiming her lips.

"You need to make love to me." Amelia pulls her face back and pins me with her no-nonsense stare.

"Are you sure it's not too soon?"

"I told you I was ready two weeks ago." She continues to stroke me, adding a bit more pressure and tightening her grip as if to emphasize her point.

"I don't want to hurt you." I will admit, watching her writhe in pain for hours upon hours did something to me. While I love our children more than air, I don't want to hurt Amelia again.

"Declan Daniel Scott, if you don't make love to me right now, I'm going to fuck my vibrator while you sit on your hands and watch. Now what will it be?"

I grin and shake my head. "I guess I'm making love to you."

Rolling her to her back, I pull her nightgown up over her head, tossing it to the ground. Her breasts are round and full, and while I never thought I was the kind of guy who would be attracted to pregnant women, my wife—perfectly round with my child—is the sexiest thing I've ever laid hands on. Gently, I kiss each nipple, running my tongue along the underside of her heavy breast as I move my hand down her body and between her legs. Over the last couple of weeks, we've mutually masturbated—her clit more plump and sensitive than before—but I've refrained from slipping my fingers inside her.

One slip of my fingers over her pussy lips and I find her wet, practically dripping with arousal. I groan, "Oh fuck, you really are ready, aren't you?"

"Yes. I would have already jumped you if I wasn't so tired all the time."

Slipping my fingers between her slick folds, I gently slide one finger inside, testing her comfort. She tosses her head back and pants, "More."

Two fingers and she's riding my hand, bucking her hips, rushing toward her climax that we're both desperate for her to have. Then, without warning, she pushes me on my back and swings her leg over my hip, lining my rock hard cock with her cunt.

"Careful, baby."

She lowers herself onto me until I'm fully seated within her hot, wet depths.

"Ah, fuck!" I hiss, my eyes rolling back, overwhelmed by pleasure. Gripping her hips, I hold her still. One, because I don't want her to hurt herself, and two, I don't think I'll last more than a couple of seconds once she moves.

Her pussy pulses softly around my cock. "Are you ready to come?"

She nods. "Yeah. I can't believe it, but I'm about to burst."

"Me too, baby. Take your pleasure. Fuck me however you want."

Amelia presses her palms against my chest and leans forward, slowly riding me in long strokes. I run my fingers into her hair and stare up at her, our eyes locked on each other. "I love you so fucking much."

Her face contorts, lips parting as her climax crashes over, her cunt milking me for my seed, which I can't stop from shooting out of my cock to paint her inner walls. Considering how fertile the two of us seem to be together, pregnancy is the first thing that comes to my mind as my brain reconnects to form rational thought.

Amelia collapses on my chest, purring her happiness. "That felt amazing."

"We should use protection for the next few months until we decide what we want to do." I blurt out.

She giggles. "Way to ruin the mood, honey."

"Sorry." I stroke my hand over her hair and then kiss her lips when she lifts her face to mock me.

"I'll talk to the doctor this week during my check-up. I don't want to take anything that will affect my breast milk."

"Understood. Whatever the safest thing to do, let me know—even if it's the old snip-a-roo."

"You'd do that?"

I shrug. "I mean, it's reversible, right?"

She also shrugs. "Supposedly. I'll talk to the doc and let you know."

"Did that hurt you at all?" I roll her to my side and face her, pulling her thigh up over my hip.

"No, it felt fantastic. When can we do it again?" She waggles her eyebrows and trails her fingers down my abs toward my already hardening cock. Apparently, she's not the only one ready for round two.

"Is this the hormones talking?" I grin.

"Absolutely. And my undying love for you." She smiles back.

Undying love—that's exactly what this is. I didn't

know I could love someone as much as I love her and my children. Whenever we fly out of town for a game, my chest tightens until I'm back home with them, where I belong. Don't get me wrong, I still love playing football. I love being a quarterback of a winning team—one set to break records again this year—but I would give it all up if that's what Amelia wanted or needed. All she'd have to do is say the word, and I'd walk away tomorrow. My ego is big, but my love for her and my family is bigger.

"Let's take a shower. I'll wash your hair and bend you over like our first morning together."

"Ah, memories." She giggles, hopping out of the way before I can smack her ass.

Memories made and a lifetime of memories to come with my big, loving family.

Also by Kameron Claire

Want more **Witty** Tongues, **Wicked** Needs, & **Wild** Deeds?

Hollywood Lights (Pre-Order)

Billionaire Romance

Show Time (Securing Selyne)

Money Shot

Three Shot

Martini Shot

Long Shot

Veteran K9 Team

Military Romance

Mine to Cherish

Mine to Crave

Mine to Possess

Mine to Adore

Mine to Covet

Mine to Worship

Mine to Protect

Mine to Treasure

Hot Nights with the Boss

** Forbidden Office / Age-Gap Romances **

Dating the Boss

Flirting with the Boss

Teasing the Boss

Tempting the Boss

Rangers Football

** Sports Romance **

Play Action Fake

Quarterback Sneak

Personal Foul

Two-Point Conversion

Red Zone

Man to Man Coverage

Short Story Collections and Bundles

Animal Attraction 4-Story Collection

Vegas Nights 4-Story Collection

Last Stand Saloon 4-Story Collection

Instalove Bundle

About the Author

USA Today Bestselling Author Kameron Claire writes stories with witty tongues, wicked needs, and wild deeds. Her books emphasize strong female leads and the protective alpha males who know how to love and support kick-ass, take-charge women. Many of her books contain military veterans, boss babes, gentle but dominant men, and goofy K9 hijinks.

Find her everywhere via linktr.ee/kameronclaire
Signed Paperbacks and discounted eBook bundles are available exclusively on her store
Subscribe to the Witty, Wicked & Wild community and read all her books online for as little as $5 a month.

www.ingramcontent.com/pod-product-compliance
Lightning Source LLC
Chambersburg PA
CBHW030147010826
48973CB00002B/760